Mills & Boon Classics

A chance to read and collect some of the best-loved novels from Mills & Boon — the world's largest publisher of romantic fiction.

Every month, four titles by favourite Mills & Boon authors will be re-published in the *Classics* series.

A list of other titles in the *Classics* series can be found at the end of this book.

Lilian Peake

MAN
OUT OF REACH

MILLS & BOON LIMITED
LONDON · TORONTO

First published 1972
This edition 1980

© Lilian Peake 1972

Australian copyright 1980
Philippine copyright 1980

ISBN 0 263 73254 1

Set in 10pt Baskerville

Made and printed in Great Britain by
C. Nicholls & Company Ltd
The Philips Park Press, Manchester

CHAPTER ONE

ROSALIE knocked on the door of her father's office, opened it and pushed her head into the room. It was empty. Disappointed, she went in, closed the door behind her and walked across to the secretary's office adjoining her father's room. That too was empty. Jane had gone home.

Rosalie sighed. After her first day in her new job she was tense with a kind of elated self-satisfaction and longed to unwind, to tell someone how much she had enjoyed herself and how much she preferred being a lecturer in a college to being a teacher in a boys' school.

But since there was no sympathetic person around to whom she could pour out her heart, she had to stifle her longing and be content with her own company for just a little longer.

She dropped her briefcase to the floor and sat in her father's swivel chair. She had always found little-girl delight in that chair. Whenever she had visited the college in the past, before becoming a member of staff herself, she had always made straight for it, swinging in abandoned circles until she was giddy. Her father had usually indulged her, giving her a few minutes to let off steam, then he would tell her to get out of it and let him sit down.

Today she was more circumspect. She sat still, resisting the temptation to whirl round, and prepared herself for a long wait. She knew her father would be late. He always was, and she had got into the habit of adding half an hour to whatever time he had promised to arrive.

She took off her jacket and draped it over the back of the chair, found the waste paper bin, saw that it was empty and turned it upside down. Then she sat in her father's chair again, removed her shoes, put her feet on the upturned bin and waited.

Feeling bored, she raked in her handbag, took out a packet of chocolate and proceeded to eat her way through it. Then she searched around her father's desk, flipped through his papers, picked up something which looked interesting, relaxed and started to read.

She was so absorbed she forgot the time, and was surprised to find that the allotted extra half-hour had gone. Growing restless and a bit irritated, she had just decided to drag herself out of her comfortable position when the door opened.

She put on a welcoming smile and started to form the words 'right on time as usual', tinged with indulgent sarcasm, when she realized with horror that it was not her father standing in the doorway, but a complete stranger.

He was tall, broadly built, and his good looks were underlined by a determination of character which added a dangerous glint to his brown eyes. He came into the room and those eyes were now staring at her as if they refused to believe what they saw. When he spoke, his voice was controlled but his annoyance was unmistakable.

'Would you mind telling me exactly what you think you're doing?'

As she watched the anger in his eyes and took in the arrogance of his whole bearing, she became acutely uncomfortable. 'What must I look like?' she wondered, and blushed a fiery red. She dropped her feet to the floor and returned the papers she had been reading to her father's desk. Then she searched frantically for her shoes, slipped them on and stood up unsteadily, feeling as though she had committed a terrible crime. In the eyes of this man, who watched all her antics in frozen silence, it seemed she had.

'I'm – I'm sorry,' was all she could find to say.

He frowned. 'Are you a new member of staff? I haven't seen you around the place before?'

'Yes. I only started today, because it's the first day of term, you see.' How feeble can I get? she thought.

He answered as though she were a five-year-old, and she felt she couldn't really blame him. 'I'm well aware of that, but what I cannot for the life of me understand is

6

how you could possibly have mistaken this room – which belongs to a head of department – for the staff common room, or even the ladies' rest room, which you evidently think you're in. Can't you read? The title on the door – Head of Department of Science and Mathematics – is surely displayed clearly enough even for someone of low intelligence to decipher. What department are you attached to?'

His cold sarcasm infuriated her and she clutched the handle of her briefcase as if it were trying to escape from her fingers. She drew in her lips and told him, 'If you must know, Business and General Studies. I'm a General Studies lecturer.'

She could hardly believe her eyes when she watched him rake in his pocket, pull out a piece of paper and write down on it the information she had just given him.

'Name?'

By now she was beginning to regain her composure and some of her usual spirit. She was not easily sat on and this occasion was no exception. 'Why should I tell him my name?' she thought. 'Does he think he can crush me with his high-handed manner because I'm a very new member of staff?'

She knew he was not the principal, nor the vice-principal, because she had met them both. So she made up her mind that she would not give any information to this overbearing individual so that he could get her into trouble – not that she had really done anything wrong. So she was silent.

'I repeat – name?'

Still she said nothing.

'Perhaps I should explain,' he said over-patiently, 'I am a senior member of staff. I am in fact, deputy head of this department.' She started at that. So this was the man her father had spoken about in such glowing terms – 'Brilliant,' he'd called him, 'he'll go a long way. Get to the top before many more years have passed.' 'As such,' he went on, 'I am responsible for the contents of this room when the department head is absent. I cannot allow anyone, and that includes you, to get away with what

7

might be described as "murder" – witness your impudent occupation of this room, your attitude when I entered, and most important of all, the fact that you were reading confidential documents which you had taken from this desk. Now will you give me your name?'

'I'm sorry, but I refuse.' After all he had said, she couldn't, simply could not tell him her relationship to the department head. Much as she disliked the man, and that was putting it mildly, she could not subject him to the embarrassment he would certainly feel if he discovered that she was the head of department's daughter.

'Very well.' He slipped the piece of paper back into his pocket. 'I have enough information already to indict you, and the fact that you won't give me your name will only make things worse for you. The fact that you're a new member of staff might count in your favour, but if I have anything to do with it, I'll make sure it will be very little in your favour. Now will you get out of here fast!'

Her cheeks scarlet with anger, she pulled on her jacket, gathered up her belongings, turned the waste bin the right way up and with a defiant stare, walked through the doorway slap into her father.

'Rosalie, my dear. I'm sorry I was so long. Did you get fed up with waiting? Come back in and wait for me. Ah, Dr. Crayford, I see you two have met.'

She stood beside her father enjoying the bewilderment and confusion on the face of the deputy head. But it soon passed and a cynical smile took its place.

'I can't wait to be formally introduced to your charming daughter, Mr. Parham.'

Franklyn Parham waved them towards each other, but their hands did not touch. Rosalie kept hers firmly round the handle of her briefcase. 'Rosalie, Dr. Crayford – er – Adrian, I think the name is? Er – Adrian, meet my daughter, Rosalie. Her first day here today. How did you get on, my dear?' He turned to Dr. Crayford. 'She's a General Studies lecturer,' he explained, smiling at his daughter, but Rosalie knew that smile. She also knew what was coming.

'Speaking as a mere scientist,' her father went on, 'Gen-

8

eral Studies teachers are, in my opinion, a necessary evil on the staff of a technical college. But my daughter knows the views of her father, don't you, dear?'

Rosalie smiled weakly. 'Only too well, Dad.' She looked at the other man. 'You, no doubt, are also one of these clever scientists, Dr. Crayford?'

'Yes, indeed, Miss Parham, I am a scientist – a mathematician like your father – but you added the word "clever". I didn't.'

'Ah, but it applies to Dr. Crayford, my dear. He's recently got his Ph.D., so don't listen to his modesty.'

Rosalie could not resist being sarcastic at the other man's expense. 'Dr. Crayford modest? You astonish me! That's a characteristic I would never have thought of applying to him.'

'Ah-ha, she has it in for you already, Dr. Crayford. You see, she lives in a family of scientists – her mother is a mathematician, too, and my daughter has acquired over the years an allergy to scientists – her words, I assure you – as a result, she says, of having the subject thrust down her throat since childhood. Although I must say I've never been aware of it.'

'I see.' The other man's eyes examined her in such detail she grew angry.

'Are we going home, Dad?' she asked, her voice dripping ice. 'I could do with a cup of tea. Somehow, I feel as though I've had enough unpleasant experiences for one day, and need reviving.'

Her father caught on to her words. 'Unpleasant experiences? Why, dear, haven't you enjoyed your first day here?'

'Very much.' She glared at Dr. Crayford and hoped he would take the hint. 'I wasn't referring to that.'

Her father snapped his briefcase shut and took her arm. 'I'll see you tomorrow, Dr. Crayford, about this collaboration we were talking about earlier.' He turned to his daughter. 'Dr. Crayford is going to help me write that maths textbook I have in mind.'

Rosalie raised her eyebrows in what she hoped was a disdainful manner. 'How very nice of him,' she murmured, and Dr. Crayford smiled at her insincerity.

Rosalie followed her father into the house, hung her jacket in the hall cupboard and went straight into the kitchen. 'Will Mum be late tonight?' she called.

Her father answered from the landing. 'No, she'll be home for tea.'

Thank goodness for an automatic cooker, Rosalie said to herself as she put on protective oven gloves and opened the oven door. The steak was bubbling in the casserole and she turned the oven knob to 'off' to allow the meal to simmer. She took the fruit jelly from the fridge and shook it free of the mould into a dish, then opened a carton of fresh cream. By the time the meal was ready to serve, her mother had come home.

Sarah Parham found her daughter in the kitchen. 'Hallo, dear,' she said, as Rosalie prepared to carry the food into the dining-room. 'You've cooked the meal, have you? That's nice of you.'

Rosalie looked at her mother, small-built, not very tall, her auburn hair only lightly touched with grey, and thought how attractive she still was although in her late forties.

Rosalie put her arms round her. 'You know I always cook it, Mum.' She rubbed her cheek against her mother's hair.

Sarah removed her daughter's arms and edged away. 'I must see your father. I want his help with a maths problem a student has asked me to solve. Where is he, upstairs?'

Rosalie nodded, frowning at her mother's lack of response, and with an effort pushed away the 'shut out' feeling she experienced whenever she thought about her.

Sarah said, 'I must wash, dear,' and went upstairs to find her husband. They were so long up there talking and laughing, that Rosalie had to call them, but still they did not come down.

What would it be like, Rosalie wondered, to have an ordinary everyday sort of mother who was not clever enough to be a university lecturer like her own mother, and who worked instead in a shop or something equally commonplace, and who showed her love without reserve?

She resigned herself to eating the first part of the meal alone. Still they talked upstairs and Rosalie knew they would be sitting on their bed, pens in hand, paper in front of them, absorbed already in the problem her mother had mentioned.

When at last they came down, they were holding hands. Once again Rosalie had to fight off the feeling of being shut out from their love and even superfluous to their lives.

'I'm an expendable commodity,' she told herself, spilling over with self-pity. 'They're so happy together they don't need me.' Then she reproached herself for even thinking it.

It was not until the meal was nearly over that Sarah remembered that Rosalie had spent her first day in her new job. 'I'm so sorry,' her mother said, 'how could I forget? Do you like it at the college better than you did at the school?'

Rosalie, delighted at last to be included in the conversation, enthused about it. 'Oh, much better, Mum. It's so different. The students are really interested in what you're teaching them, and it's much better to talk to people like that than to young boys who are forced to listen whether they want to or not.'

'She met my good friend Dr. Crayford,' Franklyn told his wife. 'Did I tell you, Sarah, now he's got his Ph.D. and has more spare time, he's agreed to collaborate with me in writing this textbook I've been thinking about?'

'How nice of him, darling. Do you think he would help with this problem I've been landed with?'

Franklyn rubbed his chin thoughtfully. 'I could ask him. He's an obliging chap.' Rosalie managed to stop herself from bursting into ironic laughter at her father's words. 'We could invite him for a meal, I suppose, and discuss the book and get him interested in this problem at the same time.'

Rosalie interrupted, 'Do let me know, Dad, when he's coming. I'll have to provide extra food, won't I?'

'I'll ask him tomorrow, dear.' Then he clicked his fingers irritably. 'Can't do it then. I've got this conference in London.' He looked at his daughter. 'You could ask him yourself, couldn't you? You've met him now.'

Rosalie frowned. If she asked him, she would have to be polite to the man, wouldn't she? But much as she disliked the idea, she had to agree. 'Which evening shall I suggest?'

'Let me see, today's Monday.' Franklyn looked at his wife. 'How about Wednesday evening, darling?'

Sarah consulted her diary. 'Fine. I'm free then. On Thursday there's a meeting of the University Academic Board I must attend. So we'll make it Wednesday. All right with you, Rosalie?'

Her daughter nodded and immediately began to think about the meal she would have to provide. She'd have to shop in the lunch hour next day, prepare the food in the evening and put it in the oven on Wednesday morning, remembering to set the oven timer to operate the cooker.

They rose from the table. 'Leave it, dear,' her mother said vaguely, 'I'll do it later.'

But Rosalie smiled. She had heard it all before. She cleared the table and washed up because she knew her mother really expected her to do it. She would not have dreamed of leaving it. Her mother and father would be shut up in the study for hours, talking about their work, and by the time they emerged, they would have forgotten all about the washing up.

Rosalie spent the evening working in her room, preparing her notes for the next day's lectures.

She met Dr. Crayford in the corridor the following afternoon. He was passing by, obviously intending to ignore her, when she plucked up sufficient courage to call his name.

He stopped in his tracks and looked at her irritably, and she thought for a moment that he had not recognized her. She hesitated, trying to word the invitation in such a way that he would see she disclaimed all responsibility for it. He said curtly, 'Yes, Miss Parham?'

She shrank involuntarily from the enmity in his eyes. Did he really dislike her as much as that?

'My – my father has instructed me to invite you to dinner tomorrow evening.'

He seemed taken aback. 'Oh, I – I don't think so, thanks. I wouldn't like to trouble your mother.'

'I think he wants to discuss the book with you, and my mother will be asking for your help, too. She's got a difficult maths problem she can't solve.' She gave him a sweet-sour smile. 'So you see, you would have to sing for your supper.'

A smile threatened to crease his face, but he had it under control immediately. The smile that had struggled to live was still-born.

'In any case,' she went on, 'you wouldn't be troubling my mother. I'm the one who cooks the meals in our house.'

'I see.' He narrowed his eyes and his expression goaded her.

'There's no need to look at me like that, Dr. Crayford. I haven't been known to poison a guest yet – even an unwelcome one. But you never know, I may make an exception of you.'

He laughed then, in spite of himself. 'All right, Miss Parham, you win. Despite, or perhaps because of the broad hint that you don't really want me, I'll risk it and accept. I'm probably too valuable to your father at the moment for you to try to get rid of me, much as you may dislike me.'

'If I do dislike you, then I've no doubt the feeling is mutual?'

It was a question he did not deign to answer. As he walked away, he called over his shoulder, 'What time shall I arrive?'

'Any time after classes close,' she answered.

Rosalie went to her father's office as usual the following afternoon to wait for him to take her home. This time she sat meekly in the corner, trying to make herself as inconspicuous as possible. She was flicking through an educational magazine she had borrowed from the college library, when the door opened and Adrian Crayford walked in. He glanced round, missed her, looked surprised, and turned to go out.

'Hallo,' she said, in a small voice, 'looking for someone?'

He jumped and scowled. Did he think she had been hiding from him deliberately?

'Yes, you. Your father's held up at a heads of department's meeting. He sent a message instructing me to take you home.' His tone of voice showed his reluctance to comply with the 'instructions'.

She picked up her briefcase and stuffed the magazine into it. With a reluctance equalling his, she followed him out and walked by his side down the stairs to the front entrance. He did not address one word to her, and he could not have made his dislike plainer if he had tried.

He opened the car door and indicated that she should get in too, then threw himself into the driving seat and drove out of the college car park. He seemed to be in a hurry.

'I'm calling at my flat first to pick up some papers your father wants,' he said shortly. 'It won't take long.'

She had to think of something to break the silence, so she said the first thing which came into her head. 'Are you married, Dr. Crayford?'

His look hit her like a glancing blow, and his tone rebuked her. 'Would I be living alone in a couple of rooms if I were?'

'Oh, possibly,' she answered airily. 'You could have a wife and family tucked away somewhere. You would expect it of a man of your age.'

'You make me sound ancient. If I had a wife, I can assure you she'd be right here at my side.' He was silent for a moment, then his lips curved into a humourless smile. 'But there's no danger of that. I'm quite content as I am – a lone wolf, living life in my own way.'

14

She couldn't help probing. 'You've never been in love?'

His answer was off-hand, as though such things did not matter. 'There was a girl once, but she preferred someone else. There's been no one since, I've taken good care of that.' The look he gave her stung her face like a sharp slap. 'No woman can penetrate my barriers again. I'm woman-proof.'

She smiled and tried to provoke him. 'Is that a warning, I wonder, or a challenge? I never could resist a challenge.'

He gave no answering smile. 'Neither, merely a statement of fact. Let's leave it at that, shall we?'

He stopped the car outside a small, modern semi-detached house in a quiet road. Rosalie was surprised. 'You live here? Is the whole house yours?'

'No. I rent the upper floor furnished – two rooms, kitchen, and use of bathroom.' He got out, and began to walk along the driveway. She wound down the car window and called after him, 'May I come in? Please?'

He hesitated, and said grudgingly after a few moments' thought, 'Well, all right, if you want to, but I won't be long. Hardly worth it for a few minutes.'

She would not be put off, so she ran after him to the front door. He opened it with his key, let her pass in front of him into the hall and she climbed the stairs.

'I warn you, everything's in one hell of a mess. I wasn't expecting visitors.'

He was right. His living-room was packed with books, magazines and papers. The breakfast crockery was standing unwashed on the table where he had hurriedly left it that morning. The atmosphere was stuffy, as though fresh air had not been allowed to circulate for weeks.

'I did warn you,' he said, when he saw her expression.

She shrugged. 'I don't condemn you. It merely awakens my feminine instincts and makes me want to get down to work.'

'You'll do no such thing,' he warned, but he softened his words with the first sign of good humour he had ever

15

shown in her presence. 'I like my mess. I'll not have a thing disturbed. No feminine hand is going to touch it. I couldn't think in a tidy atmosphere. I find it stifles me and paralyses my brain.'

They smiled at each other for the first time, and she felt a very odd sensation deep inside her. She turned quickly and walked across to a small table, piled high with books and papers. Almost hidden behind them was a photograph in a silver frame. She picked it up and looked at it while he searched for the missing papers. He found them and waited for her to join him at the door.

Instead she asked, 'Who is this lady, Dr. Crayford? Your mother?' He nodded. 'You look like her.' She compared their features. 'Same look in the eyes, same straight nose, same high cheekbones...'

He was impatiently amused. 'When you've finished analysing my facial structure, would you kindly replace the photo where you found it, then we can leave.'

Still she studied the picture. 'What's she like, your mother?'

He walked across and looked over her shoulder. 'As you can see, she's short, plump, kindly and cheerful. Unselfish and very motherly.'

'Where does she live?'

'In a small house in Middleton-in-Teesdale, County Durham. She's a widow, lives alone.' He took the picture from her and put it back on the table, first pushing aside the books and papers to let it stand upright. 'She's been educated, but she's no scholar. Why are you so interested? You'll never meet her. You're far too sophisticated to fit in there. Anyway, she's not your type.'

'Isn't she?' Her voice was dull, and as she turned to walk to the door, she could not control the quiver which passed across her mouth.

'What's the matter? Have I said something wrong?'

She made her smile deliberately brittle, and her words careless. 'Something wrong? Now how could someone as clever as you ever say anything wrong?'

He gave her a withering look as he stood back to let her go downstairs in front of him. They got into the car and he pulled away from the kerb. 'You know, I didn't invite you in. You could have stayed outside. If my mode of living has upset you, you must blame yourself for asking to see it.'

'It's not that at all. You just wouldn't understand if I told you.'

'Wouldn't I? Try me.'

'No, thank you. I never confide in ships that pass in the night, which is how I regard you.'

He pretended to wince. 'You're far too young to be so sour. How come?'

She shook her head. After a short silence, he said, 'We can't fence like this the whole evening. Shall we call a truce, a cease-fire, while I'm your parents' guest? We can return to our free-for-all when the evening's over, if you're so inclined.'

She nodded, smiled and again they were silent. Then she asked him jokingly, 'Have you reported me to my head of department yet?'

'No. I'm still thinking about it.'

Her head shot round and she stared at him. 'You wouldn't do that, would you? You're not serious?'

'I'm perfectly serious.'

'But why?' she asked him, wildly.

'Why? Look at it this way. You were in a head of department's room, and you were behaving with shocking effrontery. Suppose the principal had walked in?'

'But I was doing nothing wrong.'

'Weren't you? The position you were sitting in was an impudence in itself, not to mention the fact that you were reading something which you had taken from the desk and which might have been confidential.'

'But it was my father's room.'

'That makes no difference.'

'But I've been in there many times in the past and done silly things.'

'At those times you were just his daughter, and he probably thought fit to indulge your foolishness. Now you're a member of staff – a big difference.'

She was stunned. What could she say to make him see

her point of view? She asked, in a heavy voice, 'Would it make any difference if I said I was sorry, and that it won't happen again? It was, after all, my first day.'

It was a long time before he spoke. She looked at him, wondering if he had heard. Then she thought she detected a faint softening of his features, and her heart lifted.

'I'll think about it,' he said.

Her eyes took in the names of the streets, and she realized they were nearly home. As they approached the house, he said, 'After all, you didn't give me your name, remember.'

She looked at him with grateful eyes, and saw that he was smiling.

He followed her into the house. 'There's the lounge,' she waved him towards it, 'you can wait for my father in there.'

She went straight to the kitchen, looked at the joint and potatoes cooking in the oven and put the apple pie she had made the previous evening on the shelf above the roasting tin. She took a carton of cream from the fridge and as she tipped the contents into a jug, looked up, startled, into Dr. Crayford's amused eyes.

'M'm. It both smells good and looks good. Couldn't have done better myself.'

'You cook, Dr. Crayford? You surprise me. I never imagined an unworldly scientist would know where to start where such a down-to-earth activity as cooking is concerned.'

'No? Then how would I eat, if I didn't? I don't have a housekeeper and I certainly wouldn't employ a cook, even if I could afford to.'

She hurried past him into the dining-room, opened out the freshly-laundered cloth and spread it over the table. 'But surely you have someone to clean for you?'

He followed her from the kitchen. 'Not on your life. I told you, I won't have a woman in the place. They interfere too much.' He smiled. 'Always wanting to tidy up my mess.'

18

'Who does your washing and ironing?'

'Oh, I allow my landlady to do that, with the strict proviso that she leaves the clean stuff on the landing and doesn't go into my room.'

She looked up from setting the cutlery round the table. 'You can't mean it?'

'I can and do. So you see how privileged you were today, being allowed to put your nose into my flat, let alone the rest of your – er – elegant person.'

She gazed at him. 'But what have you got against women? What harm have they ever done to you that you can't tolerate them in your private life?'

'No harm at all, except that they're an incredible nuisance, and an irritating distraction from things that really matter.' He leaned against the door frame and looked her up and down. 'And the more attractive they are, the greater distraction they become. So I keep them out. Full stop.'

The front door opened and her parents entered the house together.

'It's just as well, Dr. Crayford, that my mother and father have arrived,' her eyes glinted with the light of battle, 'otherwise you and I might have become deeply involved in a stand-up fight about the rights and equalities of women.'

He glanced over his shoulder in the direction of the hall. 'H'm. Pity they made their entrance at that point. The discussion between us might have taken a very interesting turn.'

She left him with a frozen 'Excuse me' and greeted her parents. 'Your guest is in the dining-room, being irritating and provocative.'

They laughed and when he appeared, each in turn shook his outstretched hand.

Sarah smiled her charming smile. 'How do you do, Dr. Crayford. I'm so glad you could come. Has my daughter told you about this tantalizing problem one of my students has presented me with?'

'Hold on, dearest,' Franklyn laughed, 'let Dr. Crayford have his meal first. Otherwise I can see the food growing colder on the table than it usually does.'

Rosalie was grateful to her father. 'You won't be long, you two, will you? It's almost ready to serve.'

While her parents went upstairs to tidy themselves, she put on oven gloves and carried the dishes into the dining-room. As she dashed backwards and forwards to the kitchen, Dr. Crayford stood, hands in pockets, watching her activities with a slightly puzzled air.

'Is there anything I can do to help, Miss Parham? I feel rather foolish standing here, while you dash around as though you had a bull chasing you.'

She laughed and slowed down. 'Does it look as funny as that? No, thanks,' she answered his query, 'I'm used to this.'

'Oh,' he said, still puzzled.

During dinner, Franklyn would not allow his wife to talk shop. 'After all, we have a guest who speaks our language, unlike our daughter, so that makes three to one against her. It wouldn't be fair to Rosalie to shut her out, would it, dear?'

Dr. Crayford shot Rosalie a quizzical glance and must have seen her resentment, which increased as her father went on, 'If she had followed in our footsteps and chosen maths as her career, she would have been able to tune in to our wavelength and join in.'

His daughter tightened up and said with a stiff smile, 'Of course, Dr. Crayford, my mother didn't really want me, did you, Mum?'

'What, dear?' she answered vaguely. 'Oh, I wouldn't say that. When I discovered you were coming, I was a bit put out, but I soon got over that.'

'But you really wanted a boy,' Rosalie persisted, suddenly feeling it was essential to get a confession from her, 'a son who would follow in your and Dad's footsteps.'

Sarah's eyes floundered over her daughter's face and looked appealingly at her husband. Adrian Crayford frowned from mother to daughter and his expression registered distaste at the trend in the conversation. Then his gaze played thoughtfully over Rosalie's features, but she shut her eyes so that he would not see the pain in them.

'Rosalie,' her father pronounced with finality, leaning back in his chair, replete with the food his daughter had cooked. 'Rosalie is always trying to draw attention to herself. If it's not in what she says, which at times is outrageous, it's in the way she dresses, which is likewise. Witness the colour combination she's wearing now.'

Adrian inspected her dress. 'You mean those brilliant reds which ought to clash, but don't? Very attractive.' His eyes appraised and approved. 'Can't fault them.'

'Good heavens,' Franklyn stared at his daughter, 'Rosalie, you have an admirer.'

She bit her lip at the implication behind her father's words and began to stack the empty dishes and push them through the serving hatch. She had to give her hands something to do or she would scream.

'Leave those, dear,' her mother said. 'I'll wash them later.'

Rosalie did not answer, and went on clearing the table. Her parents invited their guest to follow them. 'We'll talk in the study. That's where we usually work.'

He lingered for a few moments, so Rosalie said, smiling defiantly, 'Flattery gets you nowhere, Dr. Crayford, especially when it's false.'

He answered quietly, 'If that's how you treat all your would-be allies, it's a wonder you have a friend in the world.'

'I don't need allies. I've done without them since the day I was born. I've learnt to walk alone.'

'Really?' His eyes were hard now. 'In that case, I'll tell you the truth you seem to want to hear. I think your choice of colours is atrocious.' And he walked out of the room.

She held back the vicious retort which sprang to her lips. He was, after all, a guest.

She filled the washing-up bowl with hot water, squeezed in some detergent and started on the dishes. She was about half-way through and her hands were deep in foamy suds when there was a sound behind her. She turned. Adrian Crayford was standing at the door. He looked round the kitchen and without a word took a tea towel and began to dry the dishes.

'There's no need, Dr. Crayford, I'm used to this.'

'As you said when I offered to help before. This time I didn't ask, so you can't refuse.'

They worked in silence for a while, then he asked, 'Why are you doing all this? I heard your mother say she would do it later.'

'That's what she always says. She never does.'

'Perhaps because you never give her the chance?'

'I'm under no illusions, Dr. Crayford. If I didn't do this now, the stuff would still be here unwashed tomorrow morning. And if I didn't prepare the evening meal in advance and set the cooker to switch on automatically, there would be no food for us when we got home.'

He persisted, 'Don't you think your mother might feel she's being pushed out of her own kitchen?'

Rosalie did not like the way the conversation was going. But his questions would not let her rest.

'Don't you think,' he went on, 'that the set-up here is largely your own fault, and you've conditioned them into using you as an unpaid housekeeper?'

Her smile was fixed as she answered, 'That's surely a "which came first, the chicken or the egg?" sort of question. I can't answer that.'

'What happens when you go out for the evening? Who feeds them?'

'I put their meal in the oven before I go out in the morning. It's ready to eat by the time they get home.'

'Then they wash up?'

'No. I do it before I go to bed.' He frowned. 'You don't believe me? I assure you I'm speaking the truth. I have a clever mother, almost brilliant, in fact. When she discovered I didn't take after her, she washed her hands of me. I've since been looked upon by my parents as an academic failure.'

'But you have a degree, surely?'

'Yes, in sociology. But whisper it, it's a dirty word in this family. It's non-scientific, you see, therefore less than

22

the dust.' She did not dare to look at him because she knew that if he had seen her eyes, he would have seen into her heart. After a while, she asked, 'Where are my parents?'

'In the study. They went into a huddle over that problem. I suggested a line of inquiry and they're following it, so I left them to it. I don't think they noticed.'

'No, I'm sure they didn't. They notice very little outside themselves when they're together. They — they love one another so much they've always shut me out.'

He stopped drying the plate he was holding, and studied her in an exasperated way. 'You know, you intrigue me....'

'I'm flattered. I didn't think you even noticed my existence.'

'Oh, I notice you, all right, if only in the way one notices an irritating gnat. In the end, it drives you so crazy, you just have to up and swat it.'

In spite of herself, she looked at him and laughed and he laughed with her. A spark of warmth kindled momentarily in their tenuous relationship.

'Tell me, Dr. Crayford, why do I intrigue you? My femininity cries out for an answer.'

'Then you can tell it to shut up. It's not your femininity I'm talking about. It doesn't mean a thing. It's irrelevant.'

She flushed and bit her lip. Once again he had slapped her down. She was used to that from her own family, but what puzzled her was why it should hurt so much when this man chose to do it.

He looked at the empty draining board. 'That all?'

'Yes. Thanks for your help.'

He hung up the tea towel, leaned against a cupboard door and watched her scour the sink. 'You intrigue me personality-wise,' he said, 'because for your age, you have the largest-sized chip on your shoulder I've ever seen. How you do wallow in self-pity! It's almost a pose, this self-denigration you indulge in. Why don't you snap out of it?'

She turned on him, her temper smouldering. 'Nobody

invited you here to act as my tame psychiatrist.'

He shrugged. 'If you don't like my opinion of you, there's one thing you can do – you can always torpedo me and watch me sink. I'm a ship and I'm passing in the night. Your words, remember.'

Her mother called, 'Dr. Crayford, where are you? We think we've solved that problem, thanks to you.'

'Just coming, Mrs. Parham. I'm in the kitchen, watching your daughter work.' He lowered his voice. 'I seem to have done nothing else since I came.'

Rosalie was in her bedroom writing out lecture notes when the telephone rang. She heard her father answer it. He called up the stairs, 'Rosalie, it's for you. Nichol.'

'Thanks, Dad.' When she went down, the study door was slightly open and she heard her father say, 'It's Rosalie's boy-friend. He's a languages teacher at the school she's just left. Not even modern languages, either. He specializes in ancient Greek and Latin. Can't stick the fellow myself.'

She walked across the hall and slammed the study door then picked up the receiver. 'Nichol? Darling, how nice to hear your voice. I'm getting on fine, thanks. Yes, it's a big change from the stuffy atmosphere of the school. Of course, the students are older and question everything, which I like. They aren't afraid to argue and give their own opinions like schoolboys.' The study door opened and Sarah went into the kitchen. 'Miss you? Of course I do. No, I haven't got another boy-friend. One at a time, you know me!' She laughed and glanced over her shoulder. She knew her voice could be heard in the study. 'When can I see you, darling? My ego's got a bit bashed lately. I need someone to appreciate me. Yes, a few kisses might help. Tomorrow evening? Yes, I'm free. Thank goodness there are only twenty-four hours in a day! 'Bye, darling, till then.'

As she replaced the receiver, her mother came out of the kitchen. She said, 'I've got the coffee going, Rosalie. If you can spare a few minutes to make it, dear . . .'

Rosalie followed her mother into the study. 'Everyone

for coffee?' Silently she challenged Adrian Crayford and he turned on a coldly assessing stare which, to her chagrin, made her colour furiously.

'Yes, dear, four coffees,' her mother said.

She made the coffee and took the tray into the study. 'I'm having mine upstairs in my room,' she said, looking at Adrian's bent head.

'All right, dear.' Her father smiled at her absently. 'It's just as well. We're talking shop, and you wouldn't understand a word of it.'

Adrian's head came up at that, and for a fleeting moment his serious eyes searched hers. A message seemed to pass between them, but it was in code and she could not find the key.

CHAPTER TWO

WHEN Nichol came the following evening, the dress Rosalie wore was a mixture of yellows, reds and purples. It was sleeveless and low-cut and shaped itself to her figure. She turned from side to side in front of the mirror and saw herself with other people's eyes. Was it just a bit garish? Was she trying to attract attention as her father had alleged? Perhaps I am, she thought, but I don't really care.

She ran a comb through her light-brown hair and it crackled as the ends sprang into soft curls. She put on some eyeshadow to add depth to her hazel eyes, and as she was finishing her make-up the doorbell chimed. She raced down the stairs to welcome Nichol, flinging the front door wide open.

'Hallo, darling,' she said, then stopped in confusion.

'Halló, Miss Parham – er – darling.' Adrian stood there, smiling blandly.

'Oh, good heavens, sorry about that,' she blurted out. 'I – I was expecting someone else.'

'So I gathered. That accounts for your look of acute disappointment.'

He eyed her dress as he stepped into the hall, but he said nothing.

'You've come to see my father?'

'Who else? Certainly not you. I wouldn't dream of being a spoilsport.'

'I don't know what you mean.'

He raised his eyebrows infuriatingly high and went into the study.

Nichol came soon after that. She led him into the lounge and he took her in his arms. 'Darling,' he said, 'it's been days. I miss you at school so much.' He kissed her gently.

She pulled away and said, 'Let's walk round the garden and talk, Nichol. I've got so much to tell you.'

26

They went out through the french windows and strolled about the lawn. The perfume of the spring flowers hung upon the air and Rosalie inhaled deeply, putting her hand in Nichol's. She was aware that all their movements could be observed from the study window which overlooked the garden. Nichol was tall and narrowly-built and she gazed up into his handsome, slightly effeminate face.

'Aren't you going to ask me how I'm getting on, darling?' she pouted playfully.

He put his hand under her chin and said soothingly, 'But of course, darling. How very remiss of me. I was absorbed in my own thoughts.'

'What's she like, Nichol?'

He started and a guilty look crept into his face.

She hung on his arm and gazed up at him. 'The girl you're dreaming about?'

He patted her hand absently. 'You know me so well, darling, you can read my mind. She – she's fabulous.'

'Who?' Rosalie was taken aback by the accuracy of her question.

'The girl who's taken over your job at school.'

'Oh.' She pulled her arm from his and he immediately put his hands on her waist and pulled her round to face him. 'Don't get jealous, sweetie. You know you're the only girl for me. As a matter of fact, she's already booked. Or so I'm told.'

She smiled up at him. 'So you've made inquiries?'

'Well, I . . .'

'You have.' They turned and walked towards the house, and Rosalie felt rather than saw watchful eyes upon them. 'Does she wear a ring?'

'No, but . . .'

'Then there's hope for you yet.'

'Don't be stupid, Rosalie.' He turned her by the shoulders and kissed her upturned mouth with unaccustomed roughness, then he gripped her hand. 'You're the girl for me and you know it.'

'Am I?' she thought, and glanced towards the study just in time to see Adrian lower his eyes from the window.

'Am I the girl for Nichol?' She was not so sure. She wasn't sure of anything any more. Nichol began to look dreamy.

'She's tall, got a good figure, black hair, beautiful face. She graduated in economics.' He stopped. 'But she's not you, is she?'

He pulled her against him and dropped a kiss on her forehead.

'It's almost as though he's playing a part – *like I am*.' The thought exploded in her brain before she could stop it. She had to get away from those watchful eyes, so she took Nichol's hand and pulled him towards the house. 'Let's go in the lounge,' she urged. 'It's boring out here.'

They sat on the couch and Rosalie edged into the corner. 'So you're not missing me at all?'

He moved sideways and slid his arm round her. 'Will you stop talking nonsense and kiss me properly?'

They were restrained at first, then a stronger feeling swept over them and she rejoiced in the sensation of being loved and wanted for herself alone. 'At least somebody appreciates me.' The thought sidled unnoticed into her mind and as they pulled apart, it did not occur to her to question the one-sidedness of it and ask herself whether she loved in return.

She listened as usual to Nichol, talking about his work, his out-of-door activities, and his opinions on everything going on in the world. As time passed, she realized she had not managed to tell him one word about her new job. He just didn't seem interested.

'Rosalie?' She heard her father's voice outside the lounge door.

'Come in, Dad. We're being very circumspect.' She added in a loud voice, hoping her words would carry to the study, 'at the moment.'

'What about some coffee, dear? Your mother will be in soon.'

She pulled her hand from Nichol's and left him exchanging a few meaningless phrases with her father. Then he followed her into the kitchen and sat and

28

watched as she prepared a tray, setting out five cups and saucers. Nichol did not offer to help as she knew Adrian would have done. He talked on, about himself and his affairs and she found her thoughts drifting away from his monotonous voice. How would Dr. Crayford react to Nichol? What would he think of her boy-friend? She had a feeling she knew just what he would say about Nichol when he had gone, and it certainly would not be complimentary.

'Five cups, darling?' Nichol's question brought her back to earth. 'Haven't you miscounted?'

'Dad has a visitor. Someone from the college who's helping him write this textbook. A mathematician, of course.'

Nichol groaned. 'Another one of *them*?'

Rosalie found herself in the odd position, for the first time ever, of wanting to defend the people Nichol was attacking.

'I bet he's ancient and learned and altogether repugnant,' Nichol was saying, 'as most of them are – er – your father excepted, of course, darling.'

'No, he's not.' She spoke more sharply than she had intended and he looked at her with surprise. 'He's quite young and – and quite pleasant, if you want to know.' She grew annoyed with herself. Why should she be standing there defending a man who irritated her beyond words, and who was rude to her almost every time they met?

Nichol's smile was twisted. 'It's like that, is it?'

'I don't know what you mean. It's not "like that" at all. If you must know, we get on each other's nerves more than I ever thought two people could. I've quarrelled with him more in the three days I've known him than with anyone else in my whole life.'

'All right, sweetie. Don't bend over backwards trying to deny it, or I'll really begin to believe those nasty suspicious thoughts that have come into my head.'

She turned on him angrily. 'Don't try to justify your wandering attentions by accusing me of having them, too.' She had to exercise the greatest self-control in carrying the tray into the lounge, to stop her shaking hands spilling the coffee all over it.

She went to the study and flung open the door. 'Coffee,' she snapped, and before the two men could raise their heads, she had shut the door again. She went back to the kitchen to find some food and saw with relief that Nichol was not there. She arranged some shortbread and chocolate biscuits on one plate and a pile of buttered scones on another and took them into the lounge, then she sat on the couch next to Nichol and poured out the coffee.

As the others appeared in the doorway, Nichol took her hand. Her father introduced the two men briefly. Dr. Crayford gave Nichol a probing glance and Rosalie had the feeling that he had summed Nichol up ruthlessly. She didn't much care to know the result of that probe.

She handed round the coffee and the food and as she bent down to give Dr. Crayford his cup, his eyes rested on hers for a brief moment. So keen and questioning was his gaze that she flushed and turned away angrily. What right had he to look at her like that? 'I haven't asked him to vet my men friends,' she fumed silently, 'and approve or disapprove as he thinks fit.'

The conversation was desultory. Rosalie knew her father did not like Nichol, and he took few pains to hide it. The front door opened and seconds later, Sarah appeared.

'Hallo, everyone.' Her eyes roamed round the room. She found her husband and smiled at him, then she withdrew her head. He was on his feet at once.

'Pour your mother a cup, Rosalie. I'll take it to her.'

She handed him the coffee and he left the room. She knew he was glad to be able to escape. He was always uncomfortable in Nichol's presence.

'Don't hurry, Dr. Crayford,' Franklyn called out. 'Take your time. I'll have a word with my wife.'

When the door closed behind him, Nichol placed his empty cup carefully on the tray, leaned back, put his arm round Rosalie and said,

'So you're another of these pestilential scientists, Dr. Crayford?'

Rosalie stared at Nichol. What was he up to? She felt a

30

surge of anxiety and closed her eyes, waiting for Dr. Crayford's angry reaction. But when she opened them again, she saw that he was smiling.

He stretched out his long legs, pushed his hands in his trouser pockets and said lazily, 'Yes, I suppose you could call us that.' He looked as though he was prepared to enjoy himself. 'What must annoy you traditionalists, who cling to the past so much – you teach Latin and ancient Greek, I believe? – is that we scientists are always asking questions.'

Nichol seemed to be caught off guard. His first shot had misfired and brought an unexpected reaction. He tried again.

'The trouble with you science bods is that you're always inventing dangerous things, and then you don't know how to control what you've invented.'

'Yes, I've heard all that before.' Dr. Crayford spoke as if he were addressing a thick-headed student. 'You see, it's not the scientists who control their inventions. Once they're off the drawing-board, most of our "dangerous inventions", as you call them, pass into the hands of the politicians and military types. And if you analyse these "dangerous" inventions you'll find that most of them were invented for specific purposes and for use at specific times. Of course a certain proportion of scientists do choose to work under military jurisdiction, but even some of those are occupied in a constructive, rather than a destructive, capacity. Anyway, it's their concern and their choice. You can't condemn all scientists for what a small number of their colleagues choose to do out of personal conviction.'

Nichol was thoughtful for a moment, then he brought up reinforcements. 'Scientists have no sense of responsibility.'

'That comes into the same category as your first statement. I've also heard this one before. A scientist's prime responsibility lies in seeking scientific truths. And it's no good my trying to explain a scientific truth to you, as you and I do not share a common language which would enable me to communicate coherently with you on the subject.'

'In other words,' Rosalie broke in angrily, 'you mean we're too dim to understand what you're talking about.'

Adrian Crayford shrugged indifferently. 'If you like to put it that way, yes.'

Nichol flushed heavily. 'Scientific types have no sensitivity, no culture.'

'Now I would regard those attributes as purely personal traits, to be found in many people, regardless of their profession or occupation.'

'There's another thing about you fellows.' Nichol was showing his bad temper now. 'Because of the danger-potential of your Machiavellian inventions, you think you can pull the strings and everyone will dance to your tune.'

Adrian merely laughed. 'That, I would say, is a viewpoint derived solely from reading too much science-fiction stuff.'

Nichol flushed again, and Rosalie knew he was struggling to keep his temper. 'Arts people like us,' he pulled her towards him possessively, 'that is, us cultural types as against you boorish technical chaps, struggle to retain the old values which you try to destroy. We do our best to preserve tradition. . . .'

'In other words,' Dr. Crayford broke in, 'what you are really saying is that, with your backward-looking attitudes, not only do you fail to make any material contribution to mankind's progress, but you actually hold it back. You arts types just talk. We act. It's the scientists and engineers – the "technical types" you sneer at, please note – who, with their "Machiavellian inventions" as you choose to call them, have made life indescribably easier for a large percentage of the world's population.'

Nichol rose. He obviously realized he had got the worst of the argument. But Adrian was determined to have the last word.

He stood, stretched in a slow, lazy fashion and put his hands behind him. 'It's my humble opinion that no one, and I mean no one, can call themselves truly cultured without some basic, elementary knowledge of science. Science deals with the future, as well as the present. With due respect, Latin and ancient Greek belong firmly in the past.'

Nichol said a brief, bad-tempered good night and stamped to the door, pulling Rosalie with him. 'Come outside and say good-bye, Rosalie. I've got to get back.'

'So early, Nichol?'

'No point in staying longer. You have visitors.'

He gave her a quick kiss on the cheek, said, 'I'll ring you some time,' and was gone.

Incensed beyond words, she flung back into the lounge and started gathering the crockery on to the tray. Dr. Crayford watched her for a few minutes.

'Sorry to have driven your boy-friend away at such an early hour.'

'You obviously did it on purpose.'

His laugh disclaimed all responsibility. '*I* did it? I like that. He introduced the subject, not I. He started on me, not the other way round.'

She knew this was true, but nothing would make her admit it openly.

'I – er – didn't notice you joining in and going to your boy-friend's defence, and arguing on his side. Could it be that, secretly, you agreed with me?'

His self-satisfied smile sickened her and she marched into the kitchen without deigning to answer. The crockery rattled and crashed together as she dropped the tray on to the kitchen table. Dr. Crayford followed.

'I take your loud silence as acquiescence.'

'Take it how you like.'

She turned both taps full on and the water cascaded into the washing-up bowl with such force that it splashed everything around, including her clothes. She dabbed at her dress with a towel, then washed the cups and saucers noisily, banging them upside down on the draining board. Dr. Crayford took a tea towel, but she turned and snatched it from him.

His eyes glittered dangerously. 'I insist,' he said, so quietly she was momentarily quelled. She gave it back to him and went on with the washing-up.

'You know,' he said thoughtfully, after a pause, 'your boy-friend intrigues me. He's what you might describe as a classic specimen,' he held up his finger and thumb as though dangling him from them, 'of an arts graduate gone to seed. His subjects belong so much to the past that he now sees the present with the eyes of someone from the past. His prejudiced ideas of science and scientists are based solely on the ignorant remarks and opinions of others, which he has accepted unquestioningly without thinking things out for himself. And if you were honest, and not so blindly prejudiced because of your own slightly unfortunate experience within your family, you would certainly agree with me.'

She turned on him. 'You're the one who reveals your ignorance and prejudice by your insensitive remarks about us non-scientists. The prime aim of the subject I teach at the technical college is to humanize scientists like you, who raise your noses in the air at the mere mention of culture.'

His eyebrows moved upwards. 'So scientists are cultural morons? Now you're copying your boy-friend and repeating, parrot-like, what you've heard others say. One day I'll make you eat your words, Miss Parham, and we'll see which of us is the more cultured.' He hung the tea towel on the rail and put his hands in his pockets. His next words, she was sure, were meant solely to provoke. He made no secret of the fact.

His smile held malice as he said, 'The chief aim in life, as I see it, of the arts and classics types like your boy-friend is to get in the hair of us scientists and by comparison to make us appreciate our own worth even more than we do already.'

She fell for his bait, and said furiously, 'No doubt you include me in that. I suppose I get in your hair?'

'You certainly do. You talk just as stupidly as he does about subjects quite outside your comprehension.'

She faced him squarely, her fists tightly clenched. 'Will you take your supercilious self out of here, Dr. Crayford, and leave me alone?'

34

To her horror, her eyes filled with tears, and he watched, astonished. 'I'm sorry.' He studied her closely and his eyes softened the merest fraction. 'I didn't intend to upset you. The veneer of hardness with which you like to cover yourself is obviously not even skin-deep. I'll try to remember that in future.' He turned at the door and smiled. 'Good night, Rosalie.'

She was beginning to settle down in her new job. Her subject, General Studies, was compulsory for all students, so every department of the technical college was represented in her classes. She discovered that, in dealing with these young people, whose home and educational backgrounds were so varied, her knowledge and imagination were stretched to a far greater degree than when she had been teaching unquestioning schoolboys.

She found the students' ideas new and challenging and class discussions were often so heated, the notes she had prepared at home were pushed aside and not even referred to. This worried her, because she was afraid that matters were getting out of control, so she decided to have a talk with her head of department, a man called Wallis Mason.

The day she went to see him, his secretary was in his office. Wallis Mason introduced them. 'Marion, this is Miss Parham, the new General Studies lecturer, daughter of Franklyn Parham, head of science and maths. Isn't that right, Miss Parham?' She nodded. 'Miss Parham, meet my valued secretary, Marion Harling. Miss Parham's name is – Rosalie, I believe?'

Rosalie smiled. 'My father must have mentioned it.'

Wallis Mason told his secretary he would call her later, and invited Rosalie to sit down. She noticed he was looking at her with interest, and something else was in his eyes which she did not care to interpret.

'Having trouble with your work, Miss Parham?'

She told him, trying not to be embarrassed by his concentrated gaze, some of her doubts and anxieties. But he put her mind at rest. He walked about the room and said, 'All this participation on the part of these students is a sign that your lectures are succeeding. It's obvious you're involving them sufficiently in the subjects you're discussing to make them want to have their say and express their own ideas.'

'I never thought of it that way,' she told him.

He sat down. 'You know, that is really the prime object of the General Studies course – to assist them individually and collectively to express themselves better and to break down the communications barrier. You may not have noticed yet how many of the young people who come to this college have something of a blind spot where self-expression is concerned. If you teachers can help them overcome this and help them become more articulate, you'll be doing society a good turn, because they will want less to express themselves destructively, like damaging other people's property, and more and more to take part in constructive debates and helping in that way to put things right.'

As she listened, she began to feel happier about her work, and realized she was on the right lines. She smiled at him and he responded with an intimate smile of his own. She tried to ignore the invitation behind it.

'What I'm beginning to do, Mr. Mason, is to formulate my own method of approach. When we're discussing the more personal aspects of the course, such as personal relationships, I hope it's allowable, but I tell them to sit round me on the floor, after pushing the tables and chairs back.'

He thought about what she had said and nodded. 'Very good idea. Unusual, perhaps, and don't be surprised if the principal raises his eyebrows if he happens to look in on one of your lectures.'

'Well, I realize it may be unorthodox, but its effect on the breaking down of the communications barrier is tremendous. Once they get down to floor level, it seems to have a liberating effect on their minds.'

He laughed. 'Only on their minds, I hope, and not in other ways, if there are any girl students amongst them!'

She knew what he meant and laughed with him. 'It

36

hasn't yet given them ideas in that direction, but I'll certainly keep a stern eye on them.'

He looked at his watch and stood up. Rosalie stood, too. 'I hope you're feeling happier now?'

'Very much, thank you, Mr. Mason.'

'Any time you need advice, just come to me. In the meantime,' he looked at his watch again, 'I see it's coffee-time. Would you – er – care to have a cup with me?'

She flushed at the question in his eyes. 'Well, I – well, yes, thank you. I would.'

He opened his secretary's door. 'We're off to coffee, Marion. Coming?'

Marion stopped typing, picked up her handbag and walked along the corridor with them. They found an empty table in the staff restaurant and Wallis Mason asked about her experiences as a teacher in a boys' school.

'It was full of tradition,' she told him, 'chained to the past. They taught ancient Greek there, not even modern Greek, and there were a lot of boys taking it. A – a friend of mine who teaches it was surprised at the number of parents who wished their sons to learn it.'

Wallis looked at her with interest. 'You think such subjects have little application to the modern world?'

'Well, they don't contribute in any way to solving the problems of the present day, do they?'

She stopped in confusion, having realized with astonishment just what she had been saying. Had she imbibed Dr. Crayford's opinions so deeply that she was beginning to adopt them as her own? She glanced round the restaurant and was horrified to discover that he was sitting at the next table, listening intently to their conversation.

He turned his head towards them as Rosalie stopped talking and his smile held gentle mockery. She stared down at her coffee cup, and tried to recover her balance. Luckily, Wallis Mason and his secretary were chatting, so she had time to pull herself together. She had not realized until that moment how much she had missed Adrian Crayford lately. She had caught sight of him now and then in the corridor and occasionally spotted him at lunch in the restaurant.

He went to her parents' house about twice a week to work on the textbook he was helping her father to write, but he never stayed to a meal. She was often out when he came, but even if she was in, she stayed in her bedroom until he had gone. For some odd reason she did not want to meet him. Instead, she wanted to hide from him.

Now she knew why. His effect on her pulse rate was devastating, and his nearness a luxury she couldn't afford too often. Her thoughts grew so chaotic she turned on the charm to her companions with such success that Wallis seemed to take it as an open invitation. She suspected that he was a man who did not need much encouragement, and the next moment her suspicion was proved correct.

'Are you busy in the evenings, Rosalie?' His voice was low as he murmured her name, his eyes pleading.

She was embarrassed and retreated at once. 'Usually fully occupied, Mr. Mason. When I'm not meeting my boy-friend,' she emphasized the words intentionally, 'I'm working on my notes at home.'

He was a little taken aback by her rebuff, but not abashed, and obviously had not given up hope of better success next time.

Dr. Crayford seemed to be aware of what was going on and turned inquiring eyes towards them. Rosalie looked at him defiantly, shouting to him silently, but unmistakably, to mind his own business.

Rosalie often had morning coffee with Marion after that. They discovered common interests and that they both loved walking. They shared an enthusiasm for Youth Hostelling, too, and decided to go walking together in the Pennines or across the Yorkshire moors.

Sometimes Wallis Mason joined them for coffee, and his interest in Rosalie seemed unfortunately to have been increased by her snub rather than the reverse.

One morning, she was sitting alone in the staff dining-room, wandering in a dream world of her own, when someone stood at her elbow and said, 'Hallo, Rosalie.'

38

She was startled out of her day-dream and looked up into a pair of brown eyes. 'Oh, hallo, Dr. Crayford.'

He sat down opposite her with his coffee. 'Repeat after me – Ad-ri-an.'

She smiled. 'Ad-ri-an.'

'Full marks. An apt pupil. I might even be able to teach you some mathematics one day.'

The words held a promise she did not dare to take seriously, because she knew the promise was false. She laughed, feeling lightheaded at his nearness. 'I doubt it. Your teaching would have to be superlative to get even elementary maths into my dim head.'

'Is that a challenge?'

'Oh no. I have enough on my plate at present, coping with my job. Thanks, though, for paying me the compliment of rating my intelligence higher than I do.'

He ladled brown sugar liberally into his cup and stirred it into his coffee. He took a sip, then said, 'I heard from your father that you've got a television set which has gone wrong.'

'Yes, it has. It's my own personal one which I keep in my bedroom. I've been meaning to contact a shop to send someone round to look at it.'

'Would I do? My charges are nominal, unlike a shop.'

'You? Do you know anything about television sets?'

'A fair amount. I know about radios, too. I'm making one of my own – a stereo radio receiver.'

'*Making* one? But that's fabulous.'

He bowed. 'Thank you.'

'But I didn't even know it was possible for any ordinary person to make one, let alone—' She stopped, confused.

'Go on. Let alone an unworldly, absent-minded, dreamy mathematician. You've obviously fallen for the stereotyped but entirely mythical image built up about us by dramatists, novelists and writers of children's comics. But to get back to what we were talking about, would you like me to have a look at your set and try to find out what's wrong with it?'

'Well, yes, please, Adrian. I'd appreciate it very much.'

39

'Don't mention it, Rosalie. A small return for the hospitality I've received at your house.'

Her pleasure dimmed at the reason he gave for offering his help.

'When shall I come? Are you free this evening? No boy-friend to entertain, for instance?'

'Not this evening.'

'What did you say his name was? Nichol?' She nodded and his eyes glinted. 'If I didn't want to spoil the unusually pleasant atmosphere which exists between us at this moment, I'd say he really ought to add the "ass" bit on the end. Very appropriate.'

He expected her to laugh, but she stood up angrily. He caught her hand and pulled her down. 'Now, now, if you walk off in a huff I won't offer my valuable services. And they're free.'

The touch of his hand on hers replaced her annoyance with a much sweeter emotion and she smiled. 'All right. This evening. Will you come to a meal?'

'Oh, I don't think so, thanks.'

'That's what you said before. My parents did tell me to say to you that you could come and go any time you wanted. They would always be pleased to see you.'

'That's very nice of them. I wonder why?'

'Oh, you probably fill that gaping hole left by the son they always wanted and never had.'

'I'd be a bit too old for that – after all, I am thirty-four.' He studied her. 'But if that were so, it would make me your adoptive brother. How would you like that?'

She made a face. 'My *brother*? Not at all, thanks. I could never look on you as a brother.'

'Really? Now, I find your reaction most interesting.'

He looked at her with half-smile full of meaning, and she moved uncomfortably. 'It's time I was going.'

He stood, too. 'Have we arranged a time?'

'You could collect me when classes are over and take me home instead of Dad. He warned me he'd be a bit late this evening.'

'Right. It's a date. Five o'clock? See you then.'

He raised his hand and was gone.

40

At five o'clock, Adrian put his head round the staff room door. 'Ready, Rosalie?'

She went over to him at once. 'You're very prompt.'

'It's a habit of mine.'

They walked to the car park and he unlocked the car door and let her into the front seat. As they turned into the main road, he asked, 'Settling into your job all right?'

'Yes, thanks. I'm enjoying it. I find it more challenging to teach young men and women, although, I must say, the ideas and opinions they hold rather shock me with their ruthlessness!'

'But surely you're not much older than they are. How old are you?'

'Twenty-four. Not so young, you see.'

He patted her hand. 'A real old lady.'

Her right hand moved to cover her left hand where his had touched her. 'I've made friends with Marion Harling.'

'Mason's secretary? She seems a nice girl. Very efficient. More so than your father's secretary. Still, we can't have everything. Jane's got looks and charm. What more could a man want?'

'Intelligence, perhaps?'

'M'm. She's got that too.' He shot a glance in her direction and must have seen her tight fists, because he smiled.

When she spoke, she tried to keep her voice under control. 'I've discovered that Marion is fond of walking, like me. We've tentatively planned a few days during the Spring Bank Holiday walking either in Derbyshire or on the Yorkshire moors.'

His eyebrows rose. 'You like walking? Surely you're too sophisticated for such open-air-girl activities. Marion, yes, but you, definitely no.'

'I'm sorry to upset your cast-iron theories about me, but you're way out about my character. I've walked hundreds of miles in my time, especially during the university vacations.'

'Have you ever been Youth Hostelling?'

41

'Often. It's great fun.' She looked at him. 'Are you going away at half-term?'

'Me? I always go to my mother's.' He didn't elaborate further. 'Here we are.' They got out of the car. 'Lead the way, Miss Parham.'

As they went up the stairs to her bedroom, she thought she ought to prepare him, so she said, feeling a bit uncomfortable, 'I wasn't expecting visitors, so I hope you'll excuse the mess.'

'Mess? I don't suppose there'll be a thing out of place.'

She laughed and threw open the door. He looked round at the books and folders strewn across the carpet, the sheets of paper which covered the bed, the armchair which had a pile of dresses and skirts draped across it. He put his hand to his head and staggered back.

'I see what you mean.' He followed her in and pretended to threaten her. 'It was you, wasn't it, who was itching to tidy up my place? It awakened your feminine instincts, didn't it? What price those instincts now?'

She backed away from him, and laughed. 'I did try to warn you. But until I saw your reaction, I didn't honestly realize just how much of a mess it is. I think one can see other people's mess, but not one's own unless you look at it through other people's eyes.'

'A feeble excuse.' He smiled as he walked across the room. 'But I'll tell you something. I like you all the better for it. It makes me feel quite at home. May I sit down?'

She rushed across and gathered up the clothes from the armchair. 'Please do.' She flung the garments on the bed. 'Would you like a cup of tea?'

'Wouldn't say no.'

'I'll go down and put the kettle on. There's the television set.'

He looked at it, frowning. 'It's rather an old model, isn't it?'

'Yes. It used to be downstairs, but my parents replaced it with a more modern one and passed the old one on to me. Will you excuse me while I make the tea?'

42

He nodded, already absorbed in his inspection. When she returned with the tea and biscuits, the back of the set was off and he was so engrossed in what he was doing, he did not seem to notice she was there. She told him that his tea was poured out, but he did not answer, although he must have heard.

She watched his fingers probing and testing, pulling and pushing. Then her eyes wandered over his broad shoulders and his thick brown hair. It had a slight wave in it and she turned away quickly and drank a gulp of tea before her thoughts got out of hand.

'Your tea's getting cold, Adrian,' she said softly, and he turned at last, wiping his hands on his handkerchief. A typical masculine action, she thought, with a rush of feeling which was by no means sisterly, then clamped down on herself at once.

'Have you found out what's wrong?'

'No. Difficult without my tools and soldering iron.'

He drank his tea and took a biscuit, his thoughts still on the television set. 'Would it be all right if I came back later and tried again when I've got my equipment with me? I've promised your father to call in anyway about the book.'

'I'll be in this evening,' she told him. 'I have my notes to prepare and some homework to mark. Any time after seven.'

He finished his tea, and went home.

Rosalie was washing up in the kitchen when her mother answered the ring at the front door. She heard Adrian's voice and felt sparks of excitement. 'Hallo, Sarah,' he said. 'Is Franklyn in?'

'So it's first names all round, is it?' she thought, squashing a ridiculous stab of jealousy.

'Where's Rosalie?' sent shock-waves of pleasure through her. 'In the kitchen washing up, as usual?'

Her mother laughed. 'That's right. Like Cinderella. I'm a terrible mother, aren't I, letting my daughter do all the work?'

'One day,' his voice came through the door, but getting

43

fainter as he moved into the study, 'I'll give her a dish-washer, with my love.'

They laughed together and the study door closed on them.

Some time later, Rosalie was sitting in her bedroom at the table under the window. All over it were books; text-books, exercise books and folders. She was making extensive notes which she hoped would see her through the next few days. She jumped at the light tap on the door.

'May I come in?'

'Yes, come in, Adrian.' There was a tool box in his hand. 'This is a new experience for me, inviting a television engineer into my bedroom.'

'Don't entice me,' he said. 'At least, not until I've done the work I've come to do.'

'The television's all yours.' She continued with her note-making.

Twenty minutes later, she asked, 'How's it going?'

The acrid smell of the soldering iron irritated her nostrils and she watched the curl of smoke rising from it as he lowered it carefully on to a block of wood which held the burning-hot blade free of the carpet. 'I think I've located the trouble. One or two disconnected wires and a couple of faulty valves. I doubt if it's more than that. I'll have to get new ones from the local shop and if they haven't got them in stock, I'll order them.' He replaced the back of the set and screwed it on tightly.

'It's good of you to take so much trouble.' She looked at her watch. 'I'll get some coffee.'

He said quietly, 'Can't your mother get it for once? After all, you're in the middle of your work.'

'If we wait for my mother to get it, we'll wait for ever.'

He started packing up his belongings and as she went out, she asked, 'Where would you like to have yours – with my parents or – or with me?'

'With you.'

She ran down the stairs, feeling strangely light-headed, and prepared two trays. The telephone rang and she answered it.

'Nichol? Oh, hallo, darling. Fine, thanks. How are you? All right for tomorrow evening? You can't make it? Why not? Oh, has she? No, I don't mind. Go and enjoy yourself. Yes, I'm free Saturday. See you then. Good-bye, Nichol.'

'So her name's Joanne,' she told herself, fighting off a feeling of dejection, 'and she's taking him home to meet her parents. He says it's nothing serious and he's only going out of curiosity. And I'll be seeing him Saturday.' Her actions became mechanical and she took her parents' coffee into the study.

'Adrian's having his with me,' she told them, ignoring their raised eyebrows. 'He's – he's still working on my set.'

She took the second tray upstairs and pushed open the bedroom door with her foot. Adrian was sitting at the table, reading her notes. He looked up and was about to speak, when he saw her face.

'What's happened?' he asked. 'Your inner light's gone out. Was that your boy-friend?'

'Yes,' she snapped.

'And he's stood you up?'

'It's no concern of yours.'

'All right. We'll change the subject. I've been reading your notes. I'm staggered at the range of subjects which they put together and for want of a better title, call it General Studies. Did you cover all this in your degree?'

'Most of it. The rest I've read up.'

'Do you really feel qualified, personally, as well as academically, to teach them this stuff about personal relationships? For instance,' he ran his finger along a line of writing, 'how to fit in with their family, how to behave with the girl- or boy-friend, how far to go in their love-making? I especially like this one: "What does being in love really mean? Is it the same as loving?" And this one: "Is there such a thing as love at first sight? Or is it physical attraction?" Well, teacher, what's the answer?'

She coloured at this loaded question and tried to side-track him away from the subject. 'Why do you have to pick on that and ignore the more important things? Look,

45

trade unions, local government, national government, the law, a study of commercial television, communities and relationships, current affairs.'

'You haven't answered my question. If you can't tell me, how can you tell your students?'

She became even more confused. 'You're quite different. Anyway,' she was standing at his side and challenged him, 'on your own admission, the only love you know anything about is filial love. So how can I talk to you about love between the sexes any more than you can talk to me about scientific truths?' She moved away and picked up her cup of coffee. 'What was it you said to Nichol that evening? – it's no good trying to explain it to you, as we don't share a common language with which to communicate on the subject.'

'Oh, well said, Miss Parham!' He applauded ironically. 'You've neatly side-stepped the whole question in a manner which would do credit to the diplomacy of a Member of Parliament being interviewed on that thing.' He nodded towards the television and stretched out his hand for a biscuit. 'But you, of course, know about all aspects of love, enough, in fact, to lecture to a group of adolescent students about it.'

She shrugged at his sarcasm and he smiled.

'You're obviously not going to be drawn.'

She was silent. Adrian drained his cup and replaced it on the saucer with a clatter. 'What I should like to know,' he persisted, 'is how you can set yourself up as a moralist when, because of your comparative youth, you cannot possibly possess the intellectual maturity to enable you to do so. I'm older than you are by ten years, yet I don't even begin to pretend to know all the answers. Anyway, if a student has a real moral problem, and many of them have nowadays, his solution of it would depend on his personality, his past experience and his family background, not on a course of lectures given by you, a young teacher and a woman at that.'

'But a chat with that teacher might just tip the scales and put him on the right lines. Anyway,' she simply had to change the subject, 'General Studies covers many other

46

things besides human relationships, as I've just pointed out. I'm sure you're ignoring all those other subjects just to prove your point.'

He merely smiled again and said nothing. There was a thoughtful silence, until she asked him, 'How long did it take you to get your doctorate?'

'A few years. I've lost count. It required total involvement, complete dedication and perseverance. I couldn't let up an inch.'

'Which might, perhaps, account for your monastic style of living?'

'Hardly. That's been through choice. You know my views on that.'

She hesitated a moment, then something inside her made her say, 'About two years after my parents married, my mother was going to start on her Ph.D., but she – she discovered I was coming, so she had to give up the idea.' She looked away from him. 'I don't think she's ever really forgiven me for being born.'

She didn't know what she had expected from him – his sympathy, probably. Certainly not the anger with which he now flailed her. 'Come off it, girl. Don't start wallowing in self-pity or I shall get up and go. I'll tell you something about my own life. I don't usually talk about myself to anybody, let alone a woman, but I'll make an exception of you.' He leaned back and crossed his legs. 'My father was a farm worker – not a farmer, a farm labourer.' He emphasized the words. 'My parents never had much money, then I came along. Two years after I was born, my father developed an illness contracted as a result of poverty and overwork. Two years after that, he died, so I've grown up virtually fatherless. My mother worked and struggled and kept us together, and made sure I got the education she was determined I would have. She was haunted by lack of money until I completed my studies and got a job. Since then, financially, she's never looked back. I've made sure of that. I've had a hard life, Rosalie, but I'm not complaining, not like you. What have you really got to grumble about – that you lack a few kisses, a few cuddles? Marry your boy-friend soon, and he'll give you all you want of those things.'

But she was scarcely listening. 'I think you've got a wonderful mother. You're very lucky.'

He stood up impatiently. 'You've quite missed the point, girl, haven't you? You're so obsessed by this imagined absence of parental affection, you're blind to everything else.' He turned at the door, hesitated and came back to stand in front of her. His expression softened as he took her hands. 'I'm convinced of one thing beyond doubt – that when you do eventually marry and have children of your own, you'll not only love them deeply, you'll show them that love without reserve. Good night, Rosalie.'

Her eyes filled with tears, and she turned her head away to hide them. He looked at her for a few moments, dropped her hands and was gone.

CHAPTER THREE

NICHOL stood on the doorstep on Saturday evening, unsure of his welcome. 'Hallo, Rosalie. Going to let me in?'

'Of course, Nichol. How are you?'

They went into the lounge and instead of joining him on the couch Rosalie sat in an armchair. He patted the cushion at his side, but she shook her head. He got up, leaned over and tried to kiss her, but she twisted her face away.

'What's the matter with you? Can't you forgive me for making a mistake?' He sat down again. 'It was – a mistake, Rosalie. I'm sorry, I must have been a fool to fall for her tactics.'

'Tactics? What do you mean?'

'She took me to meet her parents, as she promised. What she didn't tell me was that her fiancé would be there, too!'

Rosalie laughed and laughed, she couldn't help it, and Nichol looked thoroughly embarrassed. 'Oh, pack it up, Rosalie.'

At last she managed to stop, and dabbed at her eyes with a handkerchief. 'I think I can see why she did that,' she said, still laughing quietly. 'It was a wonderful way of putting you off her scent for good. You must have been pestering the life out of her.'

'Rosalie! It's not like you to talk like that. It's not true, anyway. I showed – normal interest, that's all. Why she didn't tell me the truth outright, I don't know.'

'You didn't – er – tell her the truth – that you had a girl-friend already?'

He flushed heavily. 'I'm sorry, Rosalie. Look, come and sit here, for pity's sake.' She did and he took her hand. 'Be fair, darling, you know there's not even an understanding between us, but just say the word, and I'll buy you a ring. I'm sure of my feelings now, and if you feel the same, let's

49

get married.'

'Are you proposing to me, Nichol? Because if so, I . . .'

He tutted impatiently and pulled her to him, and although she tolerated his kiss, she held herself in and wished it would end.

'What's the matter, darling?' He was put out at her lack of response. 'Can't you forgive me for one tiny lapse? Because that's all it was.'

She looked at him, and saw him with eyes which were not her own. She recalled his feeble defensive talk the evening he argued with Adrian. She remembered how Adrian had floored him time and again with infallible reasoning and how childishly irritable Nichol had grown when he realized he was beaten. She saw his weak chin and rather feminine mouth, his general air of vanity, and reminded herself of his constant interest in his own affairs to the exclusion of everything else.

'Forgive you, Nichol? There's nothing to forgive. As you say, we aren't tied to each other. We're just friends, so let's go on being friends for the time being.'

He looked distinctly relieved. 'Right, friends it is. Now, shall we go out somewhere? Let's eat first, then dance.'

She shrugged carelessly. 'Might as well. There's nothing else to do.'

So they dined and danced at the local hotel and she sighed with relief when Nichol took her home, saying he would ring her soon.

Lunches were served in the staff restaurant, and at first Rosalie had her meal with her father. Sometimes Adrian would join them, and the talk always drifted to 'shop'. This left her out in the cold, so when Marion suggested that they might lunch together Rosalie agreed immediately.

Every day at lunchtime she called for Marion and after a while, Wallis Mason joined them. He had asked Rosalie out for the evening two or three times, but she had consistently refused. Somehow, she felt she could not fully trust him, although he had never given her any reason to doubt him.

One morning Marion told her that she would not be lunching at the college in future. Her parents had bought a dog, and she would have to go home and look after him. Both her parents were out all day, and Marion was the only one in the family who worked near enough to the house to do so.

Wallis Mason murmured to Rosalie in the corridor one morning, 'Call for me at lunchtime as usual, won't you, Rosalie?' So she had called for him and they continued to lunch together, usually at a table for two. She had felt a little uncomfortable at first when eyes had followed them as they made their way across the restaurant, and those eyes had stayed on them for most of the meal. She could not understand why their movements should attract such attention, but she became hardened to the stares and shrugged them off.

One day, Wallis offered her a cigarette. 'I've never smoked before,' she laughed. 'I wouldn't know how to start.'

So he showed her how. He leaned across the table and put one between her lips. He flicked on his lighter and held it to the cigarette. He told her what to do, and at the first attempt, she got the cigarette going. They laughed together and attracted more attention than usual.

'Don't expect me to believe you've never smoked before,' he said, watching her closely. 'You smoke like a trooper.'

'Never before, honestly.' She smiled at him and he leaned forward, put his hand over hers and said quietly, 'Would you come out with me this evening, Rosalie? Please?'

She coloured slightly, and was about to refuse, but changed her mind. Why should she always put him off? Why not go out with him sometimes? Nichol was no longer interested in her, she argued, and Adrian never would be. So she made up her mind. 'Thanks, I'd like to.'

His gloating smile worried her a little. 'Dinner and dance somewhere?'

They arranged a time and as they left the restaurant

51

together, he cupped her elbow with his hand. She caught Adrian's eye and his look of disgust made her defiant and she turned to Wallis Mason, smiling at him as he walked by her side into the corridor.

She left him outside his office. 'Seven-thirty, Rosalie? I won't – come to your house, if you don't mind. Meet me at the end of your road. All right?' He raised his hand as she walked away.

That evening, she put on her multi-coloured sleeveless dress and the bright red jacket she wore over it clashed madly with some of the colours. She looked in her full-length mirror and heard Adrian whisper, 'Your choice of colours is atrocious.'

She could almost feel him staring at her, but a quick involuntary glance over her shoulder assured her that her imagination had tricked her. Why should she care what Adrian Crayford thought of her taste?

She ran down the stairs and met her parents in the hall.

'Where are you off to, dear?' her mother asked, mildly surprised.

'Dinner and dance,' she replied, slipping out of the house before the questions could begin.

'Who with?' Her father's voice followed her to the gate.

She pretended not to hear. Something held her back from telling them, and she couldn't understand why. Her father knew Wallis Mason, of course. Somehow she did not think he would approve.

'Adrian's coming this evening,' were the last words she heard as she ran down the road.

Wallis Mason's sports car was ticking over at the corner, and he welcomed her with a broad smile as he leaned across to open the door. She slipped into the car and as they pulled away, Adrian's car passed them, coming in the opposite direction. Rosalie kept her eyes averted, but knew he could not have failed to see them as his car had passed so close to Wallis's. So what? she thought. Let him see. It was no business of his.

She was determined to enjoy herself and put on a gay

mood as they dined and danced at a large hotel some way out of town. Wallis, as he had told her to call him, was a perfect host, polite, considerate and altogether charming. She forgot all the doubts she had had about him in the past. She could not fault his courteous behaviour. When he took her home, he stopped again at the end of the road. This puzzled her a little, but she decided he did not want to turn the car round in a road as narrow as the one they lived in.

He lifted his hands and turned her face towards him. 'Do it again, Rosalie, before long?' She nodded. 'May I have a good night kiss? Just one?' She nodded again. His lips were warm and gentle and he did not ask for more. As his lips lingered on hers, two or three cars passed by in both directions, but her heart was beating too fast for her to care. 'Thank you for a wonderful evening, Wallis,' she whispered.

She walked home and looked back and waved and just before she turned into the gate, he drove away.

'Hallo, dear.' Her father greeted her on the doorstep. 'You're not as late as we thought you might be. You've missed Adrian. He's just gone.'

Rosalie opened the door of her father's office the following afternoon and found it was empty. 'Late as usual,' she thought. She put her handbag on his desk, dropped her briefcase down and went across to Jane's office. She opened the door and pushed her head round it. 'Hallo,' Rosalie said cheerily, then drew back. 'Sorry. I thought you were alone.'

Adrian was leaning over the secretary, one hand on her desk, the other on the back of her chair. He was so near, his cheek was brushing her fair hair. He was watching as she typed a letter. He heard Rosalie's voice, looked over his shoulder and straightened up.

'Hallo, Rosalie. What can we do for you?' She didn't miss the 'we', and retreated quickly into her father's room.

Jane called, 'Do come in, Rosalie. There's nothing private going on in here, is there, Dr. Crayford?' Her large, little-girl eyes sought his and his voice was bordering on the intimate as he answered, 'Sh-sh, don't tell her that, Jane. If we pretend there are some secrets between us, who knows, before long, we may really have some.'

They laughed together and Rosalie's voice was toneless as she called from the other room, 'It's all right, Jane. I only wanted to have a chat while I waited for Dad.'

She sat in the swivel chair and swayed from side to side to work off the ache which had her body in its grip.

Adrian came through from the secretary's office and shut the door behind him. Rosalie kept her eyes on the pamphlet she had picked up from her father's desk and pretended to read it closely.

'At it again, Miss Parham?'

She looked up then and saw his disapproval, and flung the pamphlet down on the desk. 'Good heavens,' she snapped, 'it's nothing confidential. Look at it yourself.' She walked to the window to stare out of it unseeingly. 'I wish you wouldn't spy on me, Dr. Crayford.'

He did not reply at first and she turned to see him standing beside the desk flicking through the booklet she had thrown down. 'Spy on you?' He did not raise his eyes. 'With due respect, I wouldn't call a reprimand "spying", Miss Parham.'

She walked restlessly round the room, saying nothing and wishing her father would come back.

'I – er – was going to ask you,' Adrian put down the booklet, slipped his hands into his pockets and sat sideways across a corner of the desk, 'if it would be convenient for me to come to your house to repair your television this week-end. I've got the spare parts from the shop and can finish the job now.'

'Yes, if you like,' she answered disinterestedly. 'Which day is best for you – Saturday or Sunday?'

'When are you free?'

'Both days.'

'Really?' His raised eyebrows indicated his surprise. 'Then I'll choose Saturday. Don't overdo the enthusiasm, will you?'

That made her smile. 'Sorry if I seemed ungrateful. It's

54

very good of you to bother.'

'As you said before.' His eyes seemed to notice her list-lessness, but he made no comment.

'Ah, Rosalie.' Her father bustled in. 'Sorry I'm late again. Got caught by one of the governing body members. Hallo, Adrian.'

Adrian smiled and undraped himself from the desk. Franklyn looked at him. 'By the way, have you asked Jane about this typing we'd like her to do?'

Adrian clicked his fingers. 'As a matter of fact, I quite forgot about it.' He went to the secretary's door. 'Miss Halewood, would you honour us with your presence? Your boss and I have a favour to ask of you.'

Rosalie wandered to her father's desk, picked up the pamphlet she had been reading earlier and said, 'May I, Dad?'

'Of course, my dear. Help yourself to anything on my desk. There's nothing private there.'

She grinned at Adrian with mock-innocence. His face was a mask and almost as frightening. She rested against the windowsill and read, while the others talked. Adrian drew his chair close to Jane's and leaned near to her as he explained what they wanted her to do. They told her about the book they were writing, how they would like her to come to the house in the evenings to type the manuscript, and if she agreed, they would borrow a mathematical typewriter from the college for her use. Jane looked at Adrian and smiled.

'I'd be delighted to help you. I've never done this sort of thing before, so you'd have to tell me exactly what to do.'

'Dr. Crayford would give you all the help you need, Jane,' Franklyn assured her. 'He's very patient and his explanations are always clear. Of course, we wouldn't expect you to do this for nothing.' They discussed terms, then stood up.

'When shall I start, Mr. Parham?'

Adrian answered, 'This evening, if you're free?'

She was, so they arranged for her to arrive soon after seven.

'I'll run you home now, Jane.' Adrian's hand was resting on her shoulder. 'It's on my way. You don't live very far from me, do you?'

Adrian held the door open for her and followed her into the corridor, without once looking back. Rosalie stood disconsolately by the window watching them smile at each other as they walked away.

That evening Rosalie stayed in her room. She felt lonely and neglected. With her morale at rock bottom she needed something to comfort her, so she raked in her handbag and found the packet of cigarettes she had bought the day before. She put one in her mouth and drew it into life with the flame of a match. In between fits of coughing, (Wallis would have laughed, she thought) she tried to concentrate on her work, but her mind kept wandering away from it.

Although she strained her ears, she could not hear any sound of the typewriter, and the raised voices and laughter of the four people in the study – her mother had joined them – proved they were not in fact working at all. It's really a social gathering, she reflected, brimming over with self-pity.

The telephone rang. Adrian must have answered it, because his voice shouted up the stairs, 'Rosalie, it's Nichol-ass, your boy-friend!'

She stubbed out her cigarette angrily and went down, and had to cover her ear with her hand to shut out the noise from the study.

'Nichol? How are you? Who answered? Adrian. No, he's not keeping me company. He's helping Dad with his book. Yes, I went out last night. No, they didn't tell me you'd phoned. No, no one you know. It certainly wasn't Adrian. I never go anywhere with him. I'm not telling, Nichol. It's a secret. I'm free Friday evening. See you then.'

When she replaced the receiver, she felt Adrian brush against her arm, and it gave her a shock to find him standing so close. He was smiling sardonically. 'You certainly have a complicated love life, Miss Parham. Don't

56

get your dates crossed, will you? Remember I'm your boy-friend on Saturday. I'd hate to share you with another man.'

She turned from him impatiently. 'You'd better go back to the bosom of my family.'

He caught her chin roughly between finger and thumb and compelled her to look at him. 'Self-pity gets you nowhere, Rosalie. Nor does jealousy.'

She jerked away from him and walked up the stairs.

'Come back here,' he commanded. 'I haven't finished with you yet. I didn't come into the hall to eavesdrop on your exchange of endearments with your boy-friend.'

She stood on the stairs and muttered, 'Oh, shut up,' under her breath, but he was unmoved by her rudeness.

'I was sent to tell you – sorry, ask you – to get some coffee going. Please.'

She gave a resigned sigh and walked down to the hall, and his eyes softened slightly. 'Want any help?'

'No, thanks.'

He shrugged and returned to the study. She made the coffee and arranged some biscuits on a plate and carried the tray in to the others. Jane was at the typewriter, Adrian was standing next to her explaining something and she was gazing at him with wide-eyed innocence. He seemed to be lapping it up.

'Hallo, Jane,' Rosalie said. 'Working hard?'

Adrian raised an eyebrow, sensing the double meaning, but Jane smiled smugly. 'It's not hard work, Rosalie. Couldn't be easier.'

Sarah took the tray. 'Thank you, darling. It's very nice of you to do all this. We do appreciate it.'

She flushed with pleasure at her mother's gratitude, and felt Adrian's watchful eyes on her.

'Won't you join us, dear?'

She hesitated, looked from Jane to Adrian, and said, with decision, 'I'm working upstairs, Mum, thanks all the same,' and left them to it.

When Nichol came to the house on Friday evening he handed her a box of expensive chocolates and a cello-

57

phane-covered bouquet of flowers.

'Nichol, how lovely! But why?'

'Why shouldn't I give my best girl gifts? It shows how much I love her.'

Rosalie thought, cynically, 'There's nothing like a bit of competition to revive a man's interest,' and nearly spoke her thoughts aloud.

Nichol stood close and asked, 'Aren't you going to thank me?'

'Thank you so much, Nichol. They're lovely.'

'Don't insult me with faint praise. Thank me properly.'

She placed her gifts carefully on the hall table, and put her arms round his neck. She kissed him, but he was not satisfied. He swung her round and kissed her more fiercely than he had done for weeks. She didn't struggle because she did not want to upset him, but she didn't enjoy his embrace. He held her down and looked into her eyes, and still she submitted. The study door opened and he kissed her again.

'Is there a queue for the lady's favours?' A dry voice wafted across the hall. 'If so, I'll join it.'

They pulled apart self-consciously, and she turned in confusion to pick up her presents and hide her face from Adrian. 'Come into the lounge, Nichol. We might get a bit of privacy there.'

Adrian walked past them to the kitchen and closed the door behind him. Rosalie wondered what he was looking for in there. Something for her mother, she supposed. She and Nichol chatted for a while, then she saw the flowers lying unattended on a chair. She excused herself from Nichol and carried them to the kitchen, but stopped at the door, astonished. Adrian was getting the coffee.

He turned on her, his eyes blazing. 'What do you want? Go back to your lovesick swain. There's no need to interrupt your necking session this evening. I'm doing your work for you.'

Why was he so angry? 'I wouldn't dream of relieving you of the job,' she told him. 'I've merely come to put my lovely flowers in water.'

She found a cut-glass vase, filled it from the tap, unwrapped the flowers and carefully lowered the blooms into the water, deciding to arrange them properly later. He stood and watched, suspending all activity until she had finished.

She lifted the vase between her hands and walked to the door. She turned, saying softly, 'Thank you, Adrian, for being so thoughtful. I do appreciate it.'

She smiled and tried to put her gratitude into her eyes. But he was quite unmoved. He looked at her face framed by the flowers, then deliberately turned his back and carried on making the coffee.

All day Saturday, she had difficulty in keeping her feet on the ground. The cloud of anticipation on which she was floating cushioned her against all the usual irritations and pinpricks. After lunch, her parents left for a trip to London, and she spent some time after they had gone on a mad tidying-up spree, before getting herself ready to greet Adrian.

He was due to arrive about four o'clock, and she hoped he would spend at least a couple of hours with her. She wanted to please him so much, she was particular about her choice of clothes. In the end she wore white – matching blouse and skirt – and round her neck a large silver pendant on a long chain. The door chimes set her heart racing and his appreciative expression as she opened the door repaid in full all her efforts.

'Sweet simplicity, that's what I like,' he commented as he stepped into the hall. 'It scores every time.'

He was wearing a lightweight jacket over an open-necked shirt, and casual trousers. He looked more approachable and relaxed than she had ever seen him before. He gripped his toolbag and held under his arm a small parcel which, he said, contained the spare parts.

'May I go up?'

'You carry on,' she told him, 'while I make some tea. I expect you'd like a cup?'

'Please.'

He went up the stairs two at a time, and she put on the

kettle and arranged the crockery on the tray. She heard Adrian moving about overhead and felt a surge of happiness which left her breathless.

When she carried the tray upstairs, parts of the television set were distributed all over the carpet. She stared with horror at the mess, and he looked up and laughed at her expression.

'Afraid I can't put it all back? Just wait and see. I simply wave a magic wand and all these parts jump back on their own.'

She laughed and watched him, marvelling at his expertise. He saw the admiration in her eyes and smiled. 'You really think I'm wonderful, don't you?'

'Yes,' she answered simply.

'How I like blinding 'em with science. Once you know how to do this job, it's not really difficult. But carry on lauding me to the skies. It pleases my masculine vanity no end.'

One by one, he picked up the items strewn over the carpet and replaced them inside the set. 'You know,' he said thoughtfully, 'I might recruit myself a girl-friend after all, if only as an ego-booster. There's nothing like the bright, admiring eyes of a pretty girl to make a man feel on top of the world.' He gave her a swift, secret glance. 'Now who might I select for that exalted position? You're all tied up with a couple of boy-friends, so you won't do. Now Jane – there's a good proposition. I think she's free and heart-whole. I might work on her.'

'Your tea's cold.' She got up and went to her dressing-table, picking up a comb and frowning at her reflection, which frowned back at her with even greater ferocity. She ran the comb through her hair, for want of something better to do, then sat down at the table by the window and looked through her notes.

'Working, Rosalie, on a Saturday afternoon?'

'There's nothing else to do.'

'Doesn't my presence inspire you to think great thoughts?' He sounded as if he were smiling.

'Not especially.'

'Never mind. I've nearly finished, then I can give you

my undivided attention, and you won't feel neglected.'

'You came to see my television set, not me.'

'So I did.' He was replacing the back on the set and screwing it tightly into position when he asked, 'Where are your parents?'

'They've gone to London to a show. They won't be back until late tonight.'

He lifted the set and turned it into its correct position, switched on, stood back and waited. They watched the screen. First there came the high-pitched whistle followed by the sound. When the blank screen turned into a moving picture, proving the set was working again, she clasped her hands and said, 'Thank you so much, Adrian. It's wonderful to have it functioning again. It's been out of action such a long time.'

He turned the knobs and tuned in to the different channels. He adjusted the various buttons and eventually got a perfect picture.

'Want to watch it?'

She shook her head, so he switched off. He gathered his tools together and replaced them in his bag. As he drank his tea, she asked how much she owed him for the spare parts he had had to buy.

'Nothing. They're on me.'

'Oh, but—'

He waved her protests away. 'I must repay you and your parents somehow for the hospitality you have given me, so, as I said, I'm paying.' He stood up and dusted his hands. 'You haven't thanked me properly yet.'

'But you know I thank you, from the bottom of my heart. It was very kind of you to bother.'

He looked at her for a few seconds, then picked up his tool kit.

She frowned and her heart sank. 'Are you going already?'

'I was thinking of it. Why, don't you want me to go?'

She shook her head.

'But if I stayed, what could we do?'

She shrugged, having no answer. She had nothing to offer him, except what he clearly did not want. He had no use for a woman's love. He dropped his bag to the floor, came across and stood in front of her.

'I've got a suggestion to make. Your parents are out. You're obviously at a loose end. Would you like to come back with me for an hour or two and then you can hear something I haven't yet heard myself? I've nearly finished making that stereo radio receiver. We can share its "birth" together and if it works, you'll not only think I'm wonderful, you'll think I'm the cat's whiskers!'

She had never in her life before found it so difficult to mask her feelings, but she must have succeeded because when eventually she could control her voice enough to agree, he commented, 'You might sound a bit more enthusiastic.'

'I told you, I'd like to come. But what shall we do about food? It's five o'clock now.'

'We'll think about that later.'

She pulled on a bright red cardigan, found her handbag and she was ready. They drove through streets flooded with sunshine, and the parked cars which lined the kerbs gave it a 'Saturday' atmosphere. So he's letting me into his flat for the second time, she thought, nursing the warmth round her heart as though it were a precious baby.

'Have you tidied up your mess yet, Adrian?'

'No. As a matter of fact, it's worse than ever. You can't make a complicated piece of electrical equipment and keep the place tidy. Does that put you off?'

She shook her head. 'Nothing would put me off,' she wanted to tell him. As soon as she entered his living-room, she went across to the table and picked up the photograph of his mother. It was an enlargement of a snapshot taken in a garden. She studied it for a long time, until he came to stand beside her.

'Now, if that were a picture of me, I wonder if you would stand and gaze at it with such undisguised longing?'

She knew the answer to that question, but laughed and told him, 'You? You wouldn't be capable of all the love and affection this person is able to give.'

'Oh well, if love and affection is all you want, marry your boy-friend. No doubt, as your husband, he'll satisfy your craving.'

'Oh, but I'm not going to marry....' She stopped.

'Go on. I'm listening.'

'I'm not going to get married yet.' She grinned at him. 'But when I do, would you be my best man?'

He walked away. 'I'd love to be your best man. I might as well share your wedding since I'm never going to have one of my own.'

Still Rosalie gazed at the photograph, willing it to change from its inanimate state into pulsating life, thus freeing all the warmth and unselfish affection held captive by the glass in the picture-frame. 'Adrian, do you think you'll ever be as comfortably rotund as your mother?'

'That's a very diplomatic way of describing her stature! No. I'll take good care not to get as plump as that. In the first place I'm too active. Secondly, I won't be married, so I won't have a wife who keeps over-feeding me with carbohydrates.'

She replaced the photograph.

'Anyway,' he went on, as he raked in his tool bag, 'why are you constantly seeking affection in others as if it were your undisputed right to receive it? Doesn't it ever occur to you to give it, instead?'

'I don't know what you mean.'

'No, you wouldn't. Your obsessive belief that your parents have never loved or wanted you has unbalanced you so much you don't understand what I'm talking about.'

He went into his bedroom and pushed his way back into the living-room holding in his arms, with loving care, an elegant brown varnished wooden case. 'Here it is. Prostrate yourself in front of this work of art. It's taken me a good few months to complete.'

She looked upon it with awe as he lowered it to his dining-table.

'It's wonderful,' she commented.

He was amused. 'How do you know until you hear it?'

'Well, it looks wonderful and that's half the battle.'

'What do looks matter? It's what's inside that counts.'

'Is it?' She peered into a mirror hanging on the wall. 'There's hope for me then.'

'Stop fishing for compliments and be quiet while I put the finishing touches to this thing.'

He raked amongst the books and newspapers which littered the corners of his room and produced from the rubble two large unmounted cone-shaped speakers. As she watched him wiring them up to the radio, she experienced the first pangs of hunger. Had he forgotten about food? He was so absorbed in his task, she did not like to remind him. Anyway, for some reason, she wanted to prove that women were not the distraction he thought they were. So she sat, quiet and scarcely breathing, until he looked at her, simulating surprise. 'You still here? Good heavens, I thought you'd gone. Never knew a woman could be so quiet.'

She laughed. 'It seems you've got a lot to learn about women.'

He made no remark, but rose, lifted the speakers and placed them on chairs at equal distances from the radio receiver.

'This,' he said in a dramatic voice, 'is the moment we have all been waiting for.' He gave the equipment a final inspection and tuned to the appropriate place on the dial. 'Here goes.'

He switched on and she held her breath. The room was filled with music and she wanted to clap her hands. 'It works, it really works!'

'It certainly does.' His face was alight with achievement, and he stood beside her, lifted his arm and rested it across her shoulders. They listened together. 'It's a Tchaikovsky symphony. Do you like this sort of music? You do?' He seemed pleased.

He left her and bent down to fiddle with the controls, listening to the result of turning them on and off, this way and that. He brought the sound up until it deafened. He lowered it until it could hardly be heard. 'Plenty of power,' he murmured to himself. 'Excellent reproduction. Very sensitive. Responsive to the slightest touch. No, I'm not describing a woman,' he threw over his shoulder.

She laughed and said, 'Won't your landlady be put out at the noise?'

He stood at her side again, put his arm round her waist and listened intently to the music. 'My landlady?' he said absently. 'No, she's very long-suffering. I warned her I'd be trying this out today, anyway.'

At last the beauty of the music claimed their attention, and they stood close together and listened, emotionally now, instead of analytically. They looked at each other and his eyes raked her face.

'You know, you're very like your mother.'

She looked up at him. 'What, with my mousey hair and nondescript features? My mother's beautiful. I'm not.'

'No, you're not beautiful, but there's something about you, some indefinable quality. . . . It's your eyes, I think. Hers are warm and welcoming, whereas yours have a kind of pleading, appealing expression that – that. . . . Oh, it doesn't matter.' The music rose to a magnificent crescendo, bringing the movement of the symphony to a triumphant end. Adrian walked back to his radio and gave it his full attention. The elusive moment of shared happiness had passed.

She dared to whisper now, not wanting to disturb him, but knowing she would have to, 'Adrian, I'm – I'm getting hungry.'

He dropped everything and turned apologetically. 'I'm so sorry. I'm a terrible host, aren't I? But I've got out of the habit of entertaining young women. Well, what shall we do? Go out and eat or have a scratch meal here? I don't mind either way.'

She considered the two suggestions. 'If you've got enough bread and cold meat or cheese, I could make some sandwiches and we could have it here.'

He looked decidedly relieved. 'I was hoping you'd say that. Go into my kitchen and see what you can find. Help yourself.'

'You – you don't mind?' She could hardly believe he

was willing to give her the run of any part of his flat, let alone the kitchen.

He became impatient when he saw her hesitation and waved her away. 'Oh, get on with it, woman. What you can't find, ask for.'

So she got on with it, finding the crockery, the cutlery and the kettle. She searched for the tea caddy and teapot and found them amongst a pile of unwashed dishes. She looked for some bread, and found half a small loaf in the bread bin, but knowing it would not be sufficient for their needs, she told Adrian so.

He looked at his watch. 'Too late now to go to the shops. My landlady will help us out. Go and ask her if she can let us have some. She's got some ham and butter of mine in her fridge. And don't forget the milk. She's got that too.'

She went on to the landing, then went back. 'What's your landlady's name, Adrian?'

'Mrs. Fields.'

'So he doesn't mind if I meet his landlady.' She hugged the thought to her heart as she ran down the stairs. She tapped on the kitchen door and it was opened by a middle-aged woman with a pleasant face. Her look of astonishment was quickly checked as politeness took over. 'Yes?'

'Mrs. Fields? I'm – I'm having tea with Dr. Crayford. I've just discovered he's got hardly any bread and I'd like to make some sandwiches. He said you might be able to help.'

'Of course, dear. Come in.' She looked in her bread bin and found part of a sliced loaf. 'You can have all that, dear. I took too much yesterday. He can give it back any time. And here's his cold meat.' She opened the refrigerator door and took a packet out.

'It isn't his Sunday dinner, is it?'

Mrs. Fields laughed. 'No, I've got his joint here, too. He's not that forgetful.' She gave her some milk and butter. 'Now, is there anything else you'd like?'

'Would there be any tomatoes?'

'Of course, dear. How many, two?'

She balanced them precariously on top of the other food.

'Now if you find there's anything else you want, just let me know.'

'It's very kind of you.' As Rosalie was turning to go, a man came in from the garden.

'Jim, this is Dr. Crayford's – er – visitor.' Mrs. Fields' voice compelled him to take a good look at the young lady referred to. 'She's Miss—'

'My name's Rosalie Parham.'

'Miss Parham, this is my husband.' Rosalie nodded and smiled.

'You're a friend of Dr. Crayford, dear?'

'Yes, we – both work at the technical college in the town.'

'Oh, so you're a teacher, too?' She nodded as though that explained everything. 'Well, have a nice tea, dear. Let me know if you want anything.'

Rosalie smiled at them both and returned upstairs. Very nice people, she thought as she cleared a space on the kitchen table. She looked around and was so appalled by the mess that she decided there and then to attempt to clear it. Before Adrian could stop her she had run hot water into the sink, and had plunged her arms deep into the suds, washing the accumulated dirty dishes as fast as she could.

Two hands descended on to her shoulders and gripped them. She jumped guiltily. 'What are all these ominous feminine sounds of tidying up?'

She turned her head and looked up into Adrian's eyes, which were smiling. 'You don't really mind, do you? I had to clear a space to work on.'

'A good excuse. Yes, I do mind. You didn't come here to work. You do enough of that at home.'

He took a tea towel and started drying the dishes. 'We seem fated to do this sort of thing together almost every time we meet. I do believe that if there were a party at the college, we two would finish up in the kitchens doing precisely this.'

'I met your landlady and lord,' she told him. 'They're

very nice. They – vetted me thoroughly.'

'M'm. I guessed they might.' He looked thoughtful.

'You don't mind?'

'Not in the least.'

They finished the washing-up and Adrian returned to his radio, while Rosalie made the sandwiches. Then she went into the living-room, intending to set the table, but stopped and stared at the clutter on it.

'You – you couldn't clear it, could you?'

'No, I couldn't.'

'Well, the only other alternative is to have a sort of picnic on the floor.'

He said it suited him if it suited her. So, feeling a little silly, she spread the cloth on the carpet, stepping over it carefully to straighten the corners, and proceeded to carry the crockery and food from the kitchen and lower it to floor-level. They had their tea sitting opposite each other, Adrian on a footstool and Rosalie sitting on the floor. He looked at her and said, 'Are you sure you're having enough to eat? Just help yourself, won't you?'

'I've had sufficient, thanks. I've got to consider my figure.'

He gave her a lingering, estimating stare and said, 'There's no need to draw attention to your figure. It speaks for itself, in a loud, insistent voice.' He pulled viciously at some wires which seemed to have got caught inside a plug, and cursed loudly when they came out unexpectedly.

'It's not my fault.' It sounded ridiculous, but it was the first thing that came into her head.

'I didn't say it was, did I?'

They spoke little after that, but it was a friendly silence.

Now and then she leaned across to hand him some food, and he took it absentmindedly, his thoughts fixed on the components and wires of his radio. Once he smiled straight into her eyes, and she thought he was going to speak. She looked at him questioningly, but he shook his head. 'It'll keep,' he said, cryptically.

When they had cleared away and washed up, they returned to the living-room. She knelt beside him as he sat on the stool, and watched him working. She looked at his hands and his supple fingers, then raised her eyes to his profile and the urge to touch him was overwhelming. He looked down at that moment and caught her expression.

He paused, then deliberately, slowly, he placed the screwdriver and plug he was holding on the floor. He turned sideways and slipped his hands under her armpits. He swung her round until she was lying across him in his arms. His head came down and the kiss he took from her was uncompromising and hard. When at last they drew apart, she lay cradled in his embrace inert with shock and ecstasy. He looked down into her eyes and frowned. What he saw there seemed to disturb him beyond measure.

He lifted her up and put her from him. He picked up the screwdriver and plug and continued working. 'I'm sorry,' he said, breathing deeply, 'but you asked for that.'

She put her hands to crimson cheeks, trying to cool them. Her heart was beating at a frightening rate and she was finding it difficult to breathe. 'I didn't, Adrian,' she got out. 'I didn't!'

'Oh, but you did, my sweet. Put shutters on your eyes. They might get you into real trouble one day.'

She stood up and wandered distractedly round the room. How much had she given away? Did he know now that she loved him?

CHAPTER FOUR

His next words made the floor shake under her feet. 'How are you enjoying your affair with a married man?'

'What married man?'

'Wallis Mason, of course.'

'Wallis, *married*?' Her white face must have given him the answer he was seeking. 'You must be wrong. He would have told me.'

'So you really didn't know? I think just a little better of you for that. You're getting quite a reputation at the college, you know, going round with him.'

So that was why people had been staring at them. She remembered the niggling doubts she had had about Wallis at first, and realized now how justified they had been. 'But why didn't he tell me?'

'Either he thought you knew and you didn't care. Or he thought you did not know, and he decided not to enlighten you, in case he frightened you away.'

'But where's his wife?'

'She left him about nine months ago. Want to know why? Because he couldn't leave the women alone.'

'But he's so polite and well-behaved when we're together, I can't believe that.'

'He knows his quarry. Easy does it with you. He's clever, you know.' He looked up from his work. 'He – er – has a daughter. She's about seven. Nice little kid.'

She was aghast. 'You mean the mother left them both? Just like that?'

'Just like that. There are worse mothers than yours, aren't there?'

She felt in her handbag for cigarettes, drew one from the packet and put it between her lips. 'Mind if I smoke?'

He looked up swiftly. 'Yes, I do.'

She ignored him, searched for matches and found them. She struck one and he was across the room and had blown the match out before she knew he had moved. He pulled the cigarette from her lips and threw it away. She clenched her fists, momentarily the loser. Then she seized her handbag, drew out the packet and was about to select another cigarette when his hand closed over hers. His eyes glinted. 'How much did that lot cost?'

She told him, wondering why he wanted to know. He felt in his pocket amongst some loose change, counted out the exact amount and dropped it into her bag. Then before she had realized his intention, he had taken the packet from her fingers and pushed it into his trouser pocket.

'They're mine,' she objected furiously. 'Give them back!'

'Sorry.' His smile taunted her. 'They're mine now. I've paid for them.'

'But you don't smoke.'

'Neither do you, despite Mason's attempts to corrupt you.'

She felt so humiliated by his action that her temper got the better of her judgment. She moved quickly to his side and plunged her hand into his pocket, but his fingers caught and held her wrist in a savage grip. His will battled with hers and he conquered. She looked down at her hand, saw where it was, realized with horror how presumptuous she was being. She turned crimson, tried to move away, but found she could not. He still held her prisoner. Angry now, she tugged her wrist from his grasp and rubbed herself madly where his fingers had bruised her skin.

Tears of frustration came into her eyes. 'You can't impose your will on me like that.'

'Can't I? I'll impose my will on you in another way in a minute, if you don't behave.'

'You're quite impossible,' she snapped. 'I'm almost beginning to hate you!'

He walked away and shrugged his broad shoulders. 'It's just as well. I knew before long you'd either begin to hate me or love me. And it would be disastrous if you started to love me – there'd be no future in it. No future at all.'

71

She found she was shaking. She picked up her hand-bag, fought with the tremor in her voice and said, 'Now will you take me home?'

He looked at his watch. 'Take you home? No, it's much too early. Anyway, I'm too busy.'

She threw down her handbag and wandered round the room again.

'For goodness' sake, sit down!'

She sat down, but had to have something to occupy her distraught mind, so she got up and he tutted. She looked at the bookshelves, seized a book, sat down with her back to him, opened the book on her lap and started to cry. She couldn't see the words for crying and scrabbled in her bag for a handkerchief. Her tears were silent and secret and made blobs on the pages in front of her.

She heard him move. Then he was crouching before her, looking up into her face. He read the title of the book on her lap and smiled.

'You must be getting clever if you can understand that. Are you having secret tuition so that you can keep up with us mathematicians?'

Her eyes cleared and she saw that the book she had chosen was a textbook. She smiled tearfully.

'Mop up now,' he urged gently, giving her his handker-chief, 'otherwise I'll have to hang this book on the line to dry. Then what would my landlady say?'

He watched her dry her eyes. 'I'm sorry, Rosalie. I keep forgetting that the hard exterior you like to show the world is thinner than a coat of varnish, and that you're really very soft-centred.' He stood up and held out his hand. 'Can we be friends again?'

She put her hand in his and nodded.

'Good. Now I'll make some coffee.'

They drank it in friendly silence. He took her home later and saw her into the house, but he wouldn't go in. 'Have you enjoyed it this evening, Rosalie, apart from our little disagreement?' She nodded. 'So have I. Good night, now.'

She watched him get into his car and waved as he drove away.

Her parents were so late coming home that she was in bed before they arrived. Next morning they asked her how she had spent the time while they had been in London.

She told them, avoiding the interest in their eyes. They looked at each other, conversing silently, asking the inevitable question. She shook her head slowly. 'There's nothing more to it, you know. Nothing at all.'

But they smiled as she left them, smiled and hoped. 'I wish they wouldn't,' she thought miserably.

Next morning was Monday, and she dreaded her first meeting with Wallis Mason. At lunch-time she decided to end her class early and get to the staff restaurant before he did. She joined the queue at the self-service counter, and as she waited her turn, looked round the tables and saw her father and Adrian having their meal with other members of the science department. When she had paid for her food, she carried it across the room and stood at her father's table. Adrian looked up and smiled. 'Hallo, Rosalie. Coming to sit next to me?'

She walked round to the vacant seat beside him and he helped her unload the tray. Her father's watchful, hopeful eyes were upon them and she said, 'Hallo, Dad.'

'Hallo, stranger. Don't often have the pleasure of your company at lunch-time. You're always otherwise engaged.'

She looked at Adrian, and he said, 'She's decided on a change of air. The atmosphere is pleasanter on this side of the room.'

The others laughed and looked at her with interest and speculation. Wallis walked in, his eyes scanning the tables and he spotted her. Adrian suddenly became very attentive. He half-turned in his seat and began talking to her. She answered him automatically, not really taking in what he was saying, and he seemed to be aware of that, but he kept on talking. Her eyes roamed round the room guiltily and she saw that Wallis was scowling at her. Still Adrian talked, and she smiled at him gratefully.

When they had finished their meal, they all rose to go. Adrian went to the door with her, walked along the corridor with his arm across her shoulders. Others passed them, her father amongst them, but still Adrian's arm stayed where it was. They strolled along to the staff room and he leaned against the wall and kept her talking.

He told her his radio was giving a bit of trouble, but thought he could put it right. He told her he was going to mount his two speakers in cabinets which the building department were making for him. Interested glances came their way, but he didn't seem to care.

It came to Rosalie with some force just why he was doing it. It was his way of helping to put an end to the speculation about Wallis Mason and herself. Wallis walked past, frowning and staring openly at them. When he had gone, Adrian left her, saying, 'Will you be in to-night when I come to your house, Rosalie?' She told him she would. 'I'll see you then.' He raised his hand and went on his way.

That evening, she heard him arrive and her pulses raced.

'Rosalie working?' he asked her father as they went into the study. She wanted to run down and welcome him. She wanted to feel his arms come round her as they had on Saturday, she wanted. ... She stopped abruptly, as reality broke in. 'No future in it,' he had said. 'No future at all.'

She sobered down, calmed herself and got on with her work. She could hear their voices raised in laughter and longed to join them, her loneliness and isolation emphasized all the more by their harmony. Later in the evening, her father called upstairs, 'Will you make the coffee, Rosalie?'

She made it and took the tray into the study. Adrian asked, 'Having yours with us, Rosalie?' She hesitated and he rose from his armchair.

'Come and sit here,' he invited, and as she was about to refuse, he walked across and took her hand. He led her to his chair and sat on the arm beside her.

'Take another chair, Adrian,' her father urged. 'You can't be comfortable there.'

'No, no, Franklyn, I'm perfectly all right here.' He

74

looked down at Rosalie. 'Very comfortable, in fact.'

He handed her coffee and gave her a biscuit. He continued talking to her parents, who eyed them speculatively, as she knew they would. 'It's no use,' she wanted to tell them. 'There's nothing between us. Ask Adrian.' She half-listened to their conversation, which was mainly about the textbook they were writing. Adrian's arm stretched across the back of her chair, and now and then she could feel his fingers playing with her hair. 'Doesn't he realize,' she thought desperately, 'what impression he's giving to the two people sitting opposite? Isn't he aware of what, in their hearts, they are thinking and hoping?'

He drew her into the conversation. 'Have you told your parents, Rosalie, how we had our tea on Saturday? No? You'll never believe it,' he told them, 'but we had it on the floor!' They all laughed. 'No other woman I know would do as your daughter did. When she discovered she couldn't get the table cleared, she didn't make a great fuss, but voluntarily and literally dropped everything to floor level. We had a picnic tea on the carpet. Very enjoyable it was, too.' He looked down and they laughed together.

'She's more accommodating than I would have been,' Sarah commented.

'Oh, I don't know, dearest,' Franklyn said, 'at that stage in our relationship, we were so in love we wouldn't have noticed whether we were eating from a newspaper or a silver salver.'

Rosalie flushed at the implication, and looked at Adrian, searching his profile for the annoyance he must be feeling at the construction her father had put on their friendship. But he showed no sign of irritation; instead he looked down at her as though he liked what he had heard and as though they actually shared such a secret.

'I'll wash up these cups,' her mother said, collecting them.

Rosalie started to rise from the armchair, but Adrian held her down.

'Stay here,' he whispered. Franklyn cleared his throat, saying, 'Excuse me. I'll help Sarah,' and followed her into the kitchen.

Rosalie looked up at Adrian and asked him wildly, 'Adrian, why. . . .'

'Do you know,' he said, ignoring her question and putting his arm round her shoulders, 'my landlord thinks my girl-friend's a smasher – his very words. My landlady wants to know when we're getting married.'

She laughed uncomfortably. 'What did you tell her?'

'Oh, that we hadn't decided yet. She thought we'd make an ideal couple, both being teachers.' He stood up and walked about the room. 'I didn't enlighten her. I let her have her sweet dreams of romance. It does no harm.'

Her smile was set as she asked, 'What will you say in a few months' time when we're still no further forward?'

'Oh, that we had a quarrel and broke it off. Simple.'

He studied her face, but she made her expression blank. She glanced at the clock on the mantelpiece and rose. 'Must get back to work. Good night, Adrian.' She went to the door.

'Rosalie.'

'Yes?'

'Come back here.'

Slowly she walked across the room and stood in front of him. He cupped her face between his hands, looked deep into her eyes and kissed her. 'Good night,' he whispered.

Her legs felt so weak she wondered if she would reach the door. When she did, her parents opened it and entered. They looked at them both, then at each other, with immense satisfaction.

Rosalie avoided Wallis again the next day. She had lunch with her father and Adrian and again he behaved towards her as though they were sweethearts. Wallis had his lunch alone, and the more he scowled, the more Adrian acted the part of the boy-friend. He walked with her to the staff room door again, and they talked outside for a few minutes.

Wallis came along the corridor, stopped and looked at

his watch. 'Miss Parham,' he said in clipped, authoritative tones, 'I should like to see you in my office, please. Straight away.'

Adrian fumed when he had gone. 'He's pulling rank, Rosalie. You'll have to go. I'm sorry. I wish I could go in with you. Will you be in this evening?'

She nodded and left him. Fear stiffened her fingers as she curled them and tapped on Wallis's door. What answer should she give to the question she knew he would ask?

'Come in, Rosalie. Sit down.' He indicated a chair, fiddled with some papers on his desk, sat down and looked at her inquiringly. 'Rosalie, I'm worried. Tell me, why are you avoiding me?'

She gripped her handbag. 'It's – it's very difficult, Wallis, and I don't quite know how to say it, but – well, I've been told you're married.' It was out and even that was a relief.

'But I thought you knew. You must have heard?'

She shook her head nervously. 'I wasn't aware of the fact until last week-end. If I had known, I wouldn't have dreamed of going out with you. I'm sorry.'

'But what difference does it make? We like each other, don't we? My wife has left me. She went voluntarily, she went because she preferred another man. In due course, no doubt we shall get a divorce.'

Rosalie was astonished. 'But – but I was told she had another reason for leaving you, because. . . .'

'Because of my interest in other women?' She nodded. 'I thought so. That is a slander which is circulating about me, quite without foundation. She left me because she fell in love with another man. She left me with a young daughter to care for.' He looked down at his desk. 'And it's for her sake, Rosalie, I should like our friendship to continue. You see, she's a very unhappy little girl. Every day she asks me when her mother's coming back, every day I have to say I don't know.'

His eyes were heavy when he lifted them. 'I thought that, maybe, if you and she could get to know each other, you might come to fill that empty place in her life.'

Her heart was deeply touched by the picture he had painted of his motherless young daughter. All the same she couldn't see how she could help. 'But, Wallis, what would be the use of my getting to know her? I can't take the place of her mother.'

'My dear, I merely thought that if you would come home with me sometimes and talk to her and even play with her like her mother used to, it might help the little soul to forget for a while that her mother cared so little for her that she went away and left her.'

'Who looks after her when you're not there?'

'A neighbour. She's elderly but good-hearted and does her best.' He walked about agitatedly. 'But you're young, more in sympathy with the child.' He stood in front of her. 'Please, Rosalie, just come home and see her, then you'll understand what I mean.'

She felt trapped. Her heart went out to the little girl — she knew what it was like, she told herself, to be unloved — and longed to try and comfort her. But in the circumstances, how could she continue her friendship with Wallis? What would the other members of staff think of her? What, oh, what would Adrian think of her? Surely he would understand, wouldn't he?

Wallis saw her hesitation. He took her hand, put it to his lips. 'Please, Rosalie. I should appreciate it so much.'

She took her hand from him and tried to rub away his kiss. 'Well, I'll come and see her, but that's all I promise.'

Pleasure shot through his eyes. 'When? This evening?'

She shrugged. 'Might as well.'

'I'll call for you around seven. You can see her before she goes to bed. I'll wait in the usual place. Thanks, Rosalie,' he smiled, 'from the bottom of my heart.'

Her spirits flagged as she dressed to go out and her anxiety increased as the time approached for Adrian's arrival. She hoped to miss him, but as she ran down the stairs, the door bell chimed. She opened the door.

'Hallo, Rosalie.'

'Hallo, Adrian.' She dodged his hand which was reaching out towards her, and called to her parents, 'I'm going out. 'Bye.' She pushed past Adrian, but he caught her arm.

'I thought you were staying in this evening.' She tried to pull her arm away.

'I've changed my mind.'

'Is it Nichol?'

She shook her head and wrenched her arm from his hold.

'Who, then? Tell me.'

She ran to the gate, closed it and raced along the road. She heard Adrian walk down the path. She glanced over her shoulder and saw him leaning over the gate peering past her, and she knew he could see Wallis's car. Seconds later she heard the front door slam with such finality that it echoed and echoed in the emptiness of her heart.

Wallis leaned across and opened the car door. 'I wondered if you would change your mind, but I'm so glad you didn't.'

He described his daughter. 'She's seven, rather timid and clinging.'

'In the circumstances that's not surprising,' Rosalie commented. 'After all, with her mother gone, you're all she's got.'

'Quite. I hear her crying in the night sometimes. I go in and comfort her, but it's not the same as her mother being there.'

Wallis drove into the driveway of a modern detached house, walked round and helped her out of the car. 'She'll be next door,' he said. 'I'll go and fetch her.'

He showed her into the house and left her. Soon he was back with a pretty child with fair curls clustering about her head. Deep blue eyes looked up with suspicion and mistrust. She nestled against her father. 'When's my mummy coming home?' she asked, turning her face against his jacket.

Wallis looked at Rosalie helplessly and shook his head.

The neighbour appeared and Wallis introduced them. 'Mrs. Smith is very kind. She often puts Melanie to bed.'

Mrs. Smith eyed Rosalie with something like distaste, and she turned pink under her stare. What sort of person does she think I am? Rosalie wondered angrily. She knew, of course. 'But she's wrong,' Rosalie cried inside her. 'Like all the others, she's so wrong.'

She crouched down to the height of the child. 'Hallo,' she said. 'I'm Rosalie, and you're Melanie. Now isn't that strange, my name ends in "ie" like yours does. I think that makes us twins!'

Melanie's face started to soften into a tremulous smile, and Rosalie followed up her advantage. 'Melanie, you know your daddy works at the technical college?' She nodded. 'Well, I'll tell you something surprising. My daddy works there, too.' Her eyes widened. 'And there's something else, my daddy has a room to himself like yours.'

Melanie looked up at her father, smiled and stopped clinging to him. She turned and faced Rosalie.

'Is your daddy a head of department, too?'

Rosalie nodded. 'Do you go to the college much, Melanie?'

'Sometimes. I go to Christmas parties there.'

'Do you ever go to your daddy's room?'

'Yes. He's got a round-and-round chair.'

'So has my daddy. And shall I tell you a secret? I used to sit on that chair, even when I grew into a big girl, and go round and round until I felt giddy!'

Melanie touched Rosalie's arm, her eyes shining. 'I do that, too. Daddy swings me round so fast I have to shut my eyes. It's lovely.' She looked up at her father. 'Can we go there again soon, Daddy? I want to have a go on your chair.'

Wallis laughed indulgently and included Rosalie in the warmth of his regard. 'Soon, poppet. When I have time.'

Melanie asked, 'Rosalie, do you work there?'

'I do now.'

'Have you got a room?'

'No, I share the staff room with the other teachers. No round-and-round chair, though.' She pretended to cry.

'But you can have a go on your daddy's, can't you?'

'Of course. I forgot that.'

Rosalie stood up and noticed that Mrs. Smith was staring at her open-mouthed. 'This isn't the usual sort,' Rosalie could almost hear her thinking. 'This one's different.'

Melanie put her hand in Rosalie's. 'Would you like to come upstairs and see my dolls?'

Rosalie asked Mrs. Smith, 'Is she going to bed now? If so, may I go up with you?'

Mrs. Smith nodded. 'I'll be running her bath in while you look at her things. She's really a good little soul.'

'Is it all right with you, Wallis?'

'But of course, my dear. That's why I brought you – to make friends with my daughter.'

So they trooped upstairs and Rosalie saw all the dolls and their clothes and furniture. She admired the little pram and the dolls' house and its contents. She was allowed to go in the bathroom while Melanie had her bath, and when the child was tucked up in bed at last, and Mrs. Smith had gone home to tidy up before babysitting, Melanie took Rosalie's hand and asked, 'Will you come and play with me again soon?'

She was moved to tears at the question. She knelt down and kissed her and stroked her hair. 'I'd love to play with you again. You're such a good little playmate.'

She sighed and closed her eyes. ' 'Night, Rosalie.'

'Good night, Melanie. Sleep well.' She slipped out of the room into Wallis's arms. He held her close.

'You were marvellous, Rosalie. How can I thank you?'

Somehow she did not like to pull away from him, so she stayed where she was and shook her head. 'I did very little.'

'You did far more than you think. This is the first time for weeks she's settled down without a fuss.' He took her hands. 'Come down and have a drink with me before

Mrs. Smith comes back.'

They went into the lounge and Rosalie admired the furniture and decorations. He handed her a glass.

'Let's drink a toast: What do you say?'

Rosalie held hers up. 'To the return of Melanie's mother.'

A flicker of something very like aversion passed so quickly across Wallis's face that Rosalie thought she must have imagined it. She hoped she had, because she had to tussle severely with the doubts that swamped her at that moment.

'To the return of my darling wife,' he replied, chinking his glass against hers. He sat next to her on the couch. 'Rosalie, I feel I owe you something. Please let me take you out to dinner.'

'But I ought to go back home and do some work.'

'Work? My dear, you needn't worry about that. Your head of department won't put you on the carpet for not doing it for once!' He slipped his arm round her waist. 'And I rather like this particular member of my staff.'

He pulled her against him and she could feel his breath on her neck. She inched away from him. 'I – I don't think so, Wallis, thank you. I've had my meal. I really ought to go.'

'At least let me take you for a drink somewhere.'

She thought of Adrian at home and of his cold accusing eyes. 'I've probably let him down so badly,' she told herself miserably, 'he'll never trust me again.' 'All right,' she said aloud, 'a drink. Then I really must get back.'

When Mrs. Smith came in, Wallis took Rosalie to a quiet little pub where, he said, nobody would know them. They had a few drinks, then Rosalie looked at her watch. It was much later than she realized. She stood up. 'Please, Wallis, I really must go.'

The car park was dark, and as soon as the car doors were closed, he pulled her to him roughly. 'Kiss me before we go, darling. I insist.' His voice was thick, his breath smelt unpleasant and she closed her eyes and began to understand what Adrian had been talking about.

'Just – just one,' she murmured, hoping to humour him.

His kiss was more restrained than she had dared to hope.

'That's just a preliminary,' he whispered in her ear.

By the time they had reached the end of her road, he had sobered a little. 'Please don't say I put you off coming to see my daughter,' he said, kissing her fingers. 'Please say you'll come again soon.'

For his daughter's sake, Rosalie agreed, anxious to get out of the car. She left him and he drove away.

Adrian's car was still parked outside. Her heartbeats nearly choked her as she heard her mother call, 'Rosalie come into the study before you go upstairs, dear.'

She opened the study door. Her mother looked at her and frowned. 'Feeling tired, dear?'

Adrian's head came up from the papers he was checking and a cynical smile chased across his features. Rosalie felt she could have slapped his face.

'A bit. Did you want to see me about anything?'

'Only to say that Nichol phoned. He wanted to know if he could come tomorrow evening. I said he could, but if you were going out, you'd let him know.'

'I am going out. To Marion's. We're going to plan the route of our walking tour at half-term.'

'Oh? That sounds good, dear. Any idea where you're going?'

'Yorkshire, probably, through the dales to see the beauty spots.'

'Yorkshire? Aren't you going there at half-term, Adrian? Isn't that where your mother lives?'

He nodded without interest. 'On the border, just across the Tees.'

Franklyn smiled. 'Perhaps you'll see Adrian there.'

But Adrian immediately dismissed the possibility. 'It's very unlikely indeed. Yorkshire's a big county.'

Rosalie bit her lip. 'I'll phone Nichol. He can come the evening after next.'

She withdrew from the room and dialled Nichol's number. 'Hallo, darling.' She spoke in the loudest possible

83

voice. 'Sorry I'll be out tomorrow, but I'd love to see you Thursday.' They chatted for a few minutes, then rang off. She worked for some time in her room. When her father called up, 'Adrian's going, Rosalie,' she didn't answer. When he called again, Rosalie heard him say, 'I can't make her hear. Do you want to go up?'

'Good heavens, no,' Adrian said loudly. 'Why should I want to do that? It doesn't matter to me in the least whether she answers or not.' He wished her parents good night and drove away.

CHAPTER FIVE

THE evening Nichol came, Adrian brought Jane. Rosalie was in her bedroom working and waiting for Nichol when she heard her father welcome them in. Jane's high-pitched voice and too-eager laugh drifted up the stairs, overshadowing completely Adrian's quiet, controlled tones. He laughed at something Jane said as they all moved into the study.

When the doorbell chimed again, Rosalie raced down the stairs and greeted Nichol with a warmth which surprised even herself. She knew it was reaction, but he thought it was genuine. He caught her up and swung her round until she was laughing helplessly and begging him to put her down. Then he kissed her.

Her father put his head out of the study door. 'What's all this commotion?' he asked good-humouredly, then he saw them pull apart. 'Oh, sorry.' The door clicked shut and he said something which made them laugh. Rosalie knew he was telling them what he had seen, and experienced a pleasing sense of revenge. She took Nichol's hand and led him into the lounge, where he kissed her again.

'You know, you're a very strange girl. You blow hot and cold. One minute I think you're madly in love with me, the next I wonder if you remember I exist.'

She pulled away. 'Sorry, Nichol. I can't – really – explain it myself.'

'Never mind, it's so nice when you give me the green light that I'm willing to put up with the odd hold-ups at the crossroads.'

They talked about his work, and he passed on the gossip about different members of staff at the school. Some time later, the door opened and her father stood there.

'Are we intruding? Apparently not.' He moved into the room. 'I have a young lady here, Nichol, who is longing to meet you. Come in, my dear.' He beckoned round the door. 'This, Nichol, is my hard-working secretary, Jane Halewood. Here, Jane, is the Mr. Denton we've just been talking about. We heard you come in,' he told Nichol, 'and when I told Jane your name, she thought she had heard it before.'

Nichol had been busy all this time appraising the wide, childlike eyes, the shoulder-length hair and the nicely-rounded figure of the girl in front of him. He offered her his hand. She smiled her innocent smile and put her hand in his. 'I believe, Mr. Denton, my father's a student of yours. That is, if you're the Mr. Denton who takes French and German classes at the Adult Education Centre in the town.'

Nichol seemed to realize that he was still holding her hand. He dropped it in some confusion. Rosalie turned as she heard a muffled sound behind her and saw Adrian leaning against the doorpost, looking smug.

Franklyn backed to the door. 'I'll leave you to sort it out. Rosalie, when you're ready – coffee, dear?' She nodded.

Nichol was saying, 'I do indeed. I seem to remember a Mr. Halewood – shortish man, glasses, dark hair?'

'What there is of it,' Jane smiled at the description. 'That's my father. He'll be so interested to hear I've met you.'

Nichol indicated the couch. 'Do sit down, Miss Halewood. Tell me how he's getting on.'

Rosalie excused herself and squeezed past Adrian, who did not move an inch although he saw her coming. She gave him a withering look, but he might have been a statue for all the effect it had on him. As she prepared the coffee, she smiled grimly. So much for Adrian's girlfriend's loyalty. Like Nichol, she had a roving eye.

Adrian came to the kitchen door. 'I'll help you.'

'No, thank you.' She hoped the coldness of her voice would put him off. 'I can manage. Go back to your girlfriend.'

He gave her an odd look. 'At the moment, I'm as superfluous as you are in that lounge. So I'll give you a hand.' His tone allowed no argument. He put the crockery on the tray and found the sugar and biscuits. She was overpoweringly aware of his nearness. She lost all her defiance and turned to him, because she could not bear their silent quarrel any longer.

'Adrian,' she pleaded, but he refused to meet her eyes. 'Please will you hear what I've got to say?'

'You can talk. It doesn't mean I'll listen.'

Having got his attention, she rested her hand on his and he stood quite still. 'Will you – believe me when I say that it's for Wallis's daughter's sake I've resumed my – my friendship with him? She's such an unhappy child, longing for her mother, and I know just how she is suffering.'

He jerked away from her touch as though it stung him. '*You* know how she feels? You think *you* know, with the wonderful parents you've got? You're talking the most incredible rubbish!'

His tone was so violent she recoiled, closing her eyes because she could not stand the searing anger in his. 'Let me tell you something, Rosalie. You've let me down so badly, I feel I can't ever trust you again. I don't know why you think I'm interested in anything you do. You're under no obligation to explain your actions to me. Your affairs, and I mean that in the widest sense of the word, are your own concern, not mine. From now on, our lives are like two parallel lines, stretching into infinity, never touching, never crossing. Is that plain?'

Now her anger equalled his. 'What makes you think I've ever wanted our lives to touch? What's the use of a friend whose trust is so brittle that when someone does an act of kindness for a little child, that friend's trust cracks and gives like a – like a piece of thin ice?' He was so obviously unmoved by her words that she could not stop the tears. 'My conscience is clear and that, to me, is all that matters. If you can condemn me, without real evidence, like all the others,' she began to sob, 'then your friendship, let alone anything else, is not worth having.'

He faced her squarely. 'Look, let's get this straight. Where Wallis Mason is concerned, the path you have chosen to follow is your own business. If you have now

87

got yourself impossibly involved with a member of his family, it must have been because you wanted to do so. You could have refused to listen to his pleas and dismissed them as the subtle tricks they were. He's an old hand at finding ways of securing the services of the woman he wants.' He smiled unpleasantly. 'You must be proving just a little harder to get than all the others. But take it from me, the mousetrap is baited – the cheese, in your case, is strong stuff – his own daughter. But it all amounts to the same thing. He wants you and he's going to get you.' His features assumed the quality of marble. 'Is the coffee ready?'

He flicked a glance at her. 'You'd better do something about your face. You can't go in to the others looking like that. I'll take your parents' coffee into the study, then I'll take the other tray into the lounge. That should give you time to pull yourself together.'

The harshness of his tone stung her. She went upstairs to tidy her hair and put on some more lipstick. Then she joined the others in the lounge. Jane was sitting in an armchair and Nichol was on the couch. Adrian's cold eyes looked at Rosalie as she sat beside Nichol. She hoped that all traces of her tears had vanished, but she felt the other two would not have noticed even if she had still been crying her heart out. Adrian sat back in the armchair and observed his girl-friend and Rosalie's boy-friend as though he were watching a particularly amusing play.

Nichol was writing Jane's address in his diary. 'Tell your father I'll call and see him. If he's finding the work as difficult as that, I'd be delighted to give him some extra help.'

'That's so kind of you, Mr. Denton. You see, it's not as though he's learning these languages just for fun. He goes abroad so much on business he needs to be able to speak them. He's realized what a drawback it is to have an interpreter around all the time.' She relaxed gracefully in her seat, smiling with deep satisfaction, then turned to Rosalie. 'Will you be coming to the staff dinner-dance?'

'I'd almost forgotten about it, Jane. When is it –

88

towards the end of term? Are you going?'

'I'm taking her,' Adrian said quietly. 'She knows I don't dance, but she accepts that.'

Jane looked at him possessively. 'I'll dine with him, and that will be enough for me. It won't worry me if I sit out all the dances when I'm in such good company.'

Nichol took Rosalie's hand. 'Aren't you going to invite me, darling?'

'Of course, Nichol. I wouldn't dream of asking anyone else.'

He patted her hand. 'Rosalie dances divinely,' he told Adrian. 'You're missing something if you don't dance with her.'

'I don't doubt it,' he answered drily, 'but there are some things in life that, if you never have them, they say, you never miss.' He looked directly at Rosalie, and she knew just what he meant.

She challenged him back and shifted along the couch towards Nichol, snuggling up to him. He put his arm round her.

Adrian stood abruptly. 'Shall we go back to the study, Jane?'

'Of course, Adrian. I'm so sorry, I came to work, not to chatter. Nice to have met you, Mr. Denton.'

Nichol stood up and held out his hand. 'We'll be meeting again, Miss Halewood, won't we?' His eyes followed up his question, but before Jane could answer, Adrian had put his arm round her and taken her from the room.

Rosalie drifted back to having lunch with Wallis. She had no alternative. She could not have it with Adrian, because each time she entered the restaurant, he deliberately turned his head away.

By now, she was a frequent visitor at Wallis's home. She and Melanie were such good friends Rosalie suspected, with some anxiety, that she was beginning to take the place of her mother. Wallis often kissed her when she left him, and it worried her that his attentions were beginning to transcend the barriers she had erected between them. She sensed a certain impatience in him when she failed to respond.

Melanie had begun to rely on her so much, she was in a dilemma. For his daughter's sake, she could not stop going to Wallis's house. But she could not continue going there if his demands on her became so great she would have to break off their friendship altogether. She was beginning to suspect that he had been clever, just as Adrian had said, and that the tactics he had used on her, of moral obligation towards Melanie, had been a deliberate trap. She did not see what she could do about it, however, and just let things drift helplessly, hoping the situation would solve itself somehow.

The gulf between Adrian and herself could hardly have been wider. He barely acknowledged her. When she passed him in the corridor, he usually pretended not to see her. She felt her heart was breaking, but told herself not to be a fool. He had warned her often enough. 'I'm woman-proof,' he had said. 'I keep all women out. Full stop.' And he was being as good as his word.

One day, at lunch-time, Rosalie called in to see Marion, to wait until Wallis was free, and found she had a visitor. 'Melanie,' she held out her arms, 'how lovely to see you here!' Melanie ran to her and snuggled close.

'She's a very shy little girl,' Marion said, 'she's hardly said two words to me, have you, Melanie?'

Melanie hid her face against Rosalie's jacket. Then Wallis came in. His smile when he saw his daughter holding on to Rosalie was intimate and warm and she noticed that Marion looked away quickly. She sensed her embarrassment and felt that even her best friend was turning from her.

'As you see, Rosalie,' Wallis said, 'we have a guest for lunch. She's been away from school with a cold for the last two days, so I thought I'd give her a treat and bring her to a meal here.'

Melanie swung along the corridor between them, skipping excitedly, but when they passed through the doors of the staff restaurant, she clung tightly to their hands and looked hard at the floor. She shut out the staring eyes, the unasked question, the shock on some of the faces. So did Rosalie, who tried especially to shut out the open disapproval of her father, and the contempt in Adrian's eyes.

Melanie sat with her back to the sea of faces, and chatted non-stop. By the time they had finished, Rosalie had gone beyond the bounds of caring. She had come to terms with the despair in her heart and could only draw closer to her that veneer of hardness which Adrian had called 'not even skin deep'.

Later that afternoon, Rosalie had a free period and took Melanie on a tour of the college. She lifted her up to look through the glass panels in the doors and they saw the students at their tables and desks.

'It's just like school,' Melanie whispered, 'but aren't they big boys to go to school?'

Since some of them were grown men, with children of their own, Rosalie thought this was very funny and told her so. Melanie's eyes grew big.

'Some of them are *daddies*?' Her astonishment was even greater when Rosalie added, 'and mummies'.

'Talking of daddies,' Rosalie said, 'would you like to see my daddy?'

She nodded. 'And his round-and-round chair?'

'Of course.' Rosalie hoped her father was alone, and tapped on his door. He called, 'Come in,' and she pulled a shy little girl behind her into the room.

Adrian was there. 'I'm sorry.' She turned to go, but her father told her to stay.

'It's only that Melanie wanted to meet you.' She felt uncomfortable. Adrian's sardonic expression bored holes in her, and she wanted to run away and hide.

'Is that your daddy?' Melanie whispered, pointing.

'Yes, I'm her daddy, young lady. How do you do?' He held out his hand very seriously, and Melanie put hers into it. 'And what's your name?' She told him. 'Shall we see if we can find a sweet, Melanie?' He raked in a drawer and took out a packet of fruit pastilles. 'I always keep sweets in case a little girl comes to see me.'

Melanie took one, and Rosalie felt indescribably grateful to her father for being so friendly to her. Melanie stole a shy look at Adrian and whispered to Rosalie, 'Is that your brother?'

Rosalie laughed, and, to her amazement, so did Adrian. 'No, he's not my brother. He's a friend of my daddy's. I haven't got a brother, but I often wish I had.'

Franklyn cleared his throat and said, 'Yes, well. . . .'

Melanie went on, 'I haven't got one either. My daddy said that if I had one, I'd only fight with him.'

'That's true,' Rosalie agreed. 'Look, there's the chair.'

Melanie walked across to the swivel chair and inspected it. 'It's just like my daddy's. Does it go round and round as fast?'

'Oh, faster,' Franklyn said. 'Try it.' So she tried it, and Franklyn spun her faster and faster until she squealed with delight. Even Adrian lost his reserve and was smiling. While her father was entertaining his young visitor, Rosalie went into Jane's room. Adrian followed and stood at the window, gazing out aimlessly.

'Hallo, Jane,' Rosalie greeted her. 'Did Nichol keep his word, by the way, and give your father that extra help?'

'He certainly did, Rosalie. He's been so good.' She looked at her typewriter keys. 'He's called in quite a lot.' She raised her eyes. 'He's – he's stayed to a meal a couple of times. Didn't you know?'

'No, probably because I – er – haven't seen much of him lately.' She smiled. 'Now I know why.'

Jane searched her face. 'You don't mind?'

'Of course not.'

Adrian turned and saw for himself that Rosalie genuinely felt no resentment at her boy-friend's truancy. Then there was a heartbreaking cry from the other room.

'Where's Rosalie, *where's Rosalie gone?*' There was loneliness and terror in the child's voice and she heard her father try to calm her.

'It's all right. She's only through there.'

Adrian stared at Melanie as she stood at the door. Surely, Rosalie thought, he could see the anguish in the child's face as she searched for her and flung herself upon her, clinging as if she would never let go. Now would he understand the problem which was tearing her apart? She tried to calm the child. 'I wasn't far, was I, darling? I wouldn't leave you, poppet.'

She rested her cheek against Melanie's wet one and hugged her. She sought Adrian's eyes, and it must have been something in her expression which made him catch his breath and turn away. When Melanie was quiet, Rosalie took her hand. 'Let's go and find your daddy, darling. I've got a class.'

As she left her father's room, she thanked him for letting them in. He looked down at his blotter and doodled on it with his pen. Rosalie hoped he had seen the appeal for understanding in her eyes, and that he had read the message she was trying to convey – that her integrity was as inviolate as it always had been and that his doubts about her could be laid to rest.

When she glanced back before shutting the door, Adrian was standing with his back to her. The unaccountable stoop of his shoulders and his slightly bowed head made her want to rush back and plead with him for his forgiveness, too.

A few days later, she found Adrian alone in the staff room. He was sitting at a table reading and looked up briefly when she entered. She put her belongings on another table and walked over to him.

'Adrian?'

He looked at her as she stood beside him and looked down again. 'Yes?'

'I wondered if you could help me.' He moved impatiently, but she went on, 'The electrical equipment in room fourteen has gone wrong, and I was wondering if you could have a look at it.'

'What equipment?' Still he did not look up.

'The video tape recorder. I've been using it a lot lately to help me with my lectures, but it's not functioning correctly. It's new, so it might only be teething troubles.'

'What makes you think I'd be able to discover what's wrong? I'm not an electronics engineer. Ask one of the electrical engineering staff to have a look at it.'

'I have, Adrian, but they say they can't spare anyone.' Her voice faltered with disappointment, and he looked up at last.

He shrugged. 'You'll just have to contact the suppliers of the equipment, won't you?' He looked at her fully then. 'It's not my problem. Get someone else to help you.'

As she walked away, she realized that his eyes were unusually heavy, and his whole body seemed to be sagging with fatigue. Half-way across the room, she turned round. 'Are you feeling all right, Adrian? You look a bit off-colour.'

'Oh,' he moved his shoulders irritably, 'it's nothing. A cold, probably. If you want to know, I've got a sore throat.'

His tone told her plainly to mind her own business. Another member of staff came in, so she got on with her work.

Next morning, she went to her class in room fourteen. The students had moved the furniture out of the way and were sitting on the floor. Some of them had brought cushions, some used newspapers, while others sprawled full-length as if they were sunbathing. As soon as Rosalie appeared, they sat up and organized themselves.

She took her inflatable cushion from her briefcase and was about to blow into it when one of the students offered to do it for her. She handed it to him and he returned it to her fully inflated. 'It won't let me down suddenly when I sit on it, will it?' she asked, and they all laughed. Then she said, 'You do approve of this method of conducting my lectures? You wouldn't prefer to sit on chairs in the orthodox manner?'

They assured her they liked it much better this way, as they felt they could really get down to hard facts. Again they laughed, and she said, 'Well, we'll carry on doing this as long as we're allowed to by the powers-that-be. Just as long as the principal doesn't walk in one day!'

The door opened and her head jerked round with fright. Adrian came in and the whole class roared with

94

laughter. Rosalie put a hand to her head and held it, covering her confusion and red cheeks and trying to regain her composure.

When Adrian asked, with mild surprise, what the joke was, they told him, 'She thought you were the principal and that she would get told off for sitting on the floor.'

'Hm,' he muttered, half to himself, 'it seems to be a habit of hers to get down to floor level.'

The students laughed at his words, and he rebuked them good-humouredly, 'And I don't mean what you think I mean, either,' at which there was another burst of laughter.

Rosalie told them urgently, 'If you go on like this, the whole governing body will come in to see what's going on, let alone the principal.'

So they quietened down and Adrian said, 'Is it all right with you, Miss Parham, if I have a look at this equipment? I believe it's gone wrong?'

She unwound herself from her cushion and went over to him. 'That's very kind of you, Dr. Crayford.' She explained what had happened when she had last tried to use it, handed him the instruction booklet and left him to it.

Then she sank down to the floor and began her lecture. 'The subject I have in mind for discussion today,' she told the students, 'deals with television's place in the modern world. While you're gathering your ideas together, preparatory to talking about it, I'll give you a few of my own to consider.'

She took a deep breath and went on, 'I've recently had good cause to evaluate the place of television in my life, because my own set stopped working – it has since been repaired by a very good and valued friend of mine—' there was a clatter from the front of the room and everyone, except Rosalie, turned to watch Adrian bend to pick up a screwdriver which had unaccountably slipped from his fingers. She went on, 'It wasn't until I was without it that I appreciated its true worth. Losing the power of viewing seemed like having a window bricked up, a window through which pretty well the entire world could be seen at the flick of a switch. When that window is no longer there, one's horizon literally shrinks to the four walls of the room and the houses opposite.

'Until then, I must confess I didn't realize how important television had become in our personal lives, so important that I want you to consider how its coming has affected the population, not only of the civilized world, but also the more primitive peoples. And television itself has shown us that such people do exist even today. I want you to discuss, also, how it has broken through the barriers of language and prejudice, brought together people of widely differing outlook and background and paved the way to greater understanding between nations.'

The discussion went on for some time, with Rosalie acting as chairman, interposing a comment here and there, leading them back to the correct channels of debate when they started to stray. Now and then she gave her own opinion, and if it clashed with those of the students, asked them to explain clearly why they disagreed with her. Gradually every student was drawn into the discussion, until even the shy ones had taken part in it.

All the time she was conscious of Adrian. She could not rid herself of the feeling that he was listening to everything that was going on, and while half of her wished he would go, the other wanted him desperately to stay. At last, he walked over to her and she scrambled up and faced him. Her cheeks were flushed with the heat of the debate, and although she tried, she could not take the brightness out of her eyes because he was there beside her. His gaze flickered over her appreciatively and her heart began to pound unmercifully.

'Excuse the interruption, Miss Parham,' he spoke formally, 'but I think I've discovered what's wrong with this thing.' She followed him across to the video tape recorder and he started to explain the technicalities. While she understood what he was saying at first, he soon became too technical and she lost track completely. He must have sensed this by her response and said quietly, 'You understand, of course, everything I'm saying?'

Her eyes searched anxiously and she saw the gentle

curve of his lips. She replied, smiling back at him, 'But of course, Dr. Crayford, I understand every word.'

She knew the whole class was watching them, and could hear what they were saying, and one of the young men jumped up and said, 'Explain it to me, sir, I understand about tape recorders.'

'So do I,' another said, and half a dozen students surrounded Adrian, asking him to tell them what was wrong.

He looked at Rosalie apologetically. 'Sorry. Do you mind?'

She shook her head. 'Call it part of general studies,' she answered, resigning herself to handing over the class to him for the remaining ten minutes. She saw then what a good teacher he was, how patiently he explained the details to the students, how painstakingly he told them, using technical terms with which most of them seemed familiar, how it would need repairing.

'Don't I take you for maths?' he asked one of them.

'Yes, sir, that's right. I'm an electrical engineering student.'

'So am I, sir, you take me, too.'

There was a chorus of 'and me, sir', and Adrian laughed and said, 'Well, I shall expect a great improvement in your maths work now, as a way of thanking me for teaching you some electronics.' He looked at his watch. 'Now, I must tender my sincere apologies to Miss Parham for virtually wrecking her lecture. I'd better make myself scarce before she batters me with her inflatable cushion.'

They all laughed as he gathered up his belongings. The students began to drift out of the classroom to their next lecture, and Adrian told her, 'Now I've discovered what's wrong with the equipment, Miss Parham, I'll pass on the information to the electrical department, and they can send a member of staff along to repair it. It won't take them so long to do the job now.'

'It's very good of you, Dr. Crayford. Thank you for coming to look at it.' The classroom was empty now and as he turned to go, she said, 'Adrian.'

He stopped on his way to the door. 'Yes?'

She scanned his face. 'You still don't look well. How's your throat?'

He gave a half-smile. 'Why are you so worried? It's not your problem. But you're right, I still don't feel too good. Throat's still sore, got odd aches and pains.'

'Shouldn't you see a doctor?'

'Oh, women! No, I should not see a doctor. Next week's half-term, as you know, and I'm going north at the week-end. My mother will give me all the looking-after I need.' He walked away, then turned back and said, 'But thanks for your concern, Rosalie. I appreciate it.'

It was Friday evening and the college had closed for half-term. It coincided with the Spring Bank Holiday, and Rosalie's parents had already left for their week in Scotland. She was joining Marion on Sunday morning for their walking tour in the Yorkshire dales. Although she was looking forward to the break from routine, she hated the thought of the days that would have to pass before she saw Adrian again.

She had not seen him to say good-bye. He had gone home early and she had missed him. Wallis had said he was taking Melanie to his mother's for the week. Nichol had rung to wish her a good journey. He had not said when he would contact her again, and it hurt her a little that he could forget about her so easily – it hurt her pride, nothing more.

She lay in bed that night and wondered how she could cut Adrian from her heart. Her love for him was so firmly embedded that she knew it would take major surgery to tear it out. She remembered the ecstasy of his kisses, and then began to wonder why he had let her into his life for a brief period. Had she imagined that he was developing deeper feelings for her? She pommelled the pillow and tried to get comfortable, and decided she must have done. Lately he had not been even a friend, let alone a lover. She turned over, made believe that she was in Adrian's arms, and drifted into sleep.

She awoke next morning unrefreshed and restless. Soon

after breakfast, the telephone rang. She picked up the receiver. 'I'm sorry to trouble you,' the voice said in her ear, 'but does a Miss Parham live there?'

'Rosalie Parham speaking.'

'Oh, thank goodness for that! I don't know whether you remember me, but I'm Mrs. Fields, Dr. Crayford's landlady.'

'Yes, of course, Mrs. Fields, I remember you well.'

'I'm so glad I've managed to find you, dear. I found your name in the phone book and took a chance on it being your number, only Dr. Crayford isn't at all well. He's in bed, and I've had the doctor to him, although he said he didn't want one. The doctor said he's got a virus and it's gone to his lungs and he's got a temperature and a terrible cough. The point is, dear, I can't keep looking after him as I've got my own hubby, you see, and you're the only young lady I've ever known him to be friendly with and have visit him, and his mother lives too far away. So what I was wondering, dear, is whether you could come and look after him. Is it asking too much?'

'Of course not, Mrs. Fields. I'll come round as soon as I've organized things here. Does he know you've phoned me?'

'No, he doesn't, dear. He keeps saying he doesn't want anyone, but honestly, he looks so ill, he's got to have someone with him in case he gets worse.'

'Right, I'll be along straight away.'

When Mrs. Fields had rung off, Rosalie phoned Marion. 'I'm terribly sorry,' she told her, 'but I won't be able to join you tomorrow for our walking tour.'

Marion sounded upset. 'But why, Rosalie? We had it all planned.' Rosalie told her why. 'But must it be you?' she persisted.

That was difficult. 'Well, he's been helping Dad with this book they're writing, on top of all his other work, so I feel obliged to go and look after him in case we're partly to blame for his illness.'

She knew it was not true, but Marion seemed to accept it. 'I'll go north on my own and visit some relatives up there. I haven't seen them for years.'

Rosalie apologized again and rang off.

Rosalie knocked on Mrs. Fields' front door and wondered fearfully what her reception would be. Would Adrian order her out, would he welcome her or would he not even notice she had come? She would soon know.

Mrs. Fields let her in.

'Did you tell him I was coming?' Rosalie asked her.

'No, dear. He's been asleep and I didn't want to wake him. You go up and if there's anything you want, come down and tell me. If I haven't got it, my hubby can always get it, like he got Dr. Crayford's medicine from the chemist.'

Rosalie went upstairs and put her things in the living-room, then she opened Adrian's bedroom door and went in. At first he was asleep, but she must have disturbed him because he opened his eyes and stared. He looked worse than she thought he would.

'Rosalie? What are you doing here?' Even his voice was feeble.

'I've come to look after you.'

He stirred restlessly. 'I don't want looking after. You can go home.'

'I'll go when you're better, Adrian.'

'Go now. I don't want you here.'

She bit her lip and walked to the door. Then he started coughing, and when he had finished, he lay back exhausted. She sat on his bed and put her hand over his. 'Is there anything you want?'

He shook his head. 'Why did you come?'

'Mrs. Fields asked me to.'

He turned his head away.

'Would you like any food?' He didn't answer. 'Or a drink?'

He turned on his side and his very action dismissed her, so she tiptoed out and closed the door. She had put on slacks before leaving home, and she tied round her waist the apron she had brought with her. She went into the kitchen and stood quite still for a moment, refusing to accept the chaos there.

Unwashed dishes were piled in the sink and on the draining board. A half-used loaf of bread was standing on the table next to an empty milk bottle. A teapot, used but still containing the tea leaves, stood guard over the chaos and she saw it as a challenge. So she dealt with that first, and, having got started, carried on from there.

It took her some time to make any headway, but she succeeded at last in restoring some sort of order to the place. Then she began to clean. Using a cloth and scouring powder, she brought a shine to greasy surfaces, scrubbed the sink and draining board and mopped the dusty windowsill.

It was nearly midday before she crept into Adrian's room again. He was awake, but lying quite still. He watched as she approached.

She smiled. 'Now will you have some milk?'

'If you like.' His indifference increased her anxiety.

'Hot or cold?'

'Warm.'

So she heated some milk and took it in, helping him into a half-sitting position and handing him the cup. He drank it slowly, silently, taking with it the tablets the doctor had prescribed. She watched him all the time, and he closed his eyes as if to shut hers out. 'Are you feeling any better?'

'Not much.'

He gave her back the empty cup and slid down under the bedclothes.

'Do you want to sleep again, Adrian?'

'Yes.' So she left him and started with a will on the living-room. She hung up his jacket which he had obviously pulled off and thrown down when he had arrived home from the college, feeling too ill to care. She straightened the cushions on the armchairs and dusted wherever it was possible to dust, in between books and speakers and radio parts.

She found some notes he had been preparing and left unfinished. They were incomprehensible to her, but she pored over them, wishing she could understand at least some of the writing, and thus share a common language with him and be able to talk to him on his own level. She sighed and, finding nothing else to do, took off her apron and stared out of the window. It was a beautiful day in late May. Children were playing in the street below. Some older boys wheeled round and round on their bicycles and shouted to each other; now and then a car passed.

She thought about Melanie and her longing for her mother. She thought about herself and her longing for Adrian. She thought about Adrian, lying there, lifeless, uncaring, so different from the vital, energetic man he usually was.

She heard him coughing and went quickly into his room. She sat on his bed and gave him a box of paper tissues. He gasped for breath and instinctively she put her arm round him as though he were a child in need of comfort. And somehow, his head was cradled against her breast and she was holding him close. He stayed there for a long time as if loath to move, then she lowered him to the pillows.

'Sorry, Rosalie.' He whispered the words, and his eyes sought hers.

'It's all right, darling. I don't mind. I only wish I could do something to help you.' Then she realized what she had said. Her hand went to her mouth. Had he noticed? He gave a weak smile and groped for her hand. As he took it, he whispered, 'Do you call all your men patients "darling", nurse?'

'No,' she whispered back, 'only the very special ones.'

'So I'm special, nurse?'

'Very,' she said. She closed the door quietly and left him.

It was then that she realized she hadn't eaten since breakfast, so she looked round the kitchen for some food, and found a tin of meat and a bag of tomatoes. Would he mind, she wondered, if she helped herself? She went in to him, but he was asleep, and as she gazed down at his face, she noticed the stubble growing on his cheeks and the way his long eyelashes curved. Her eyes dwelt on his pleasant mouth which he had once laid on hers.

She escaped to the kitchen and decided to help herself and buy replacements in a day or two. As the hours passed, she thought about going home. She found the landlady in the kitchen.

'Would you mind, Mrs. Fields, if I didn't go home to-night? I thought if I could sleep on the couch in Adrian's living-room. . . .'

'You know, dear, I'd be glad if you would, just in case he wanted something and I didn't hear him call. I don't mind a bit. What about telling your people where you are?'

'Oh, they're in Scotland, so that won't matter. I'll look round for some sheets and blankets in Adrian's cupboards.'

'If you can't find any, let me know, and I'll give you some of mine. Would you like to use my folding bed?'

'Oh, no, thanks. The couch will do. There's one thing, though. . . .'

'You'd like to borrow a nightie? Of course, I'll lend you one. Not exactly glamorous, but that won't matter, will it? You're not on your honeymoon yet!'

So we are engaged, are we? she thought. She shrugged as she went upstairs. Perhaps it was better that she should believe that, in the circumstances. She helped Adrian into the bathroom, and while he was there she made his bed. She searched in his cupboards for bed linen and found a pillow, two sheets and a blanket and even an old eiderdown tucked away at the back. Before he saw what she was doing, she took them into the living-room.

'You'd better go home,' he told her later. 'There's no need for you to come tomorrow.'

She shook her head as she tucked him in, but said nothing. Despite the discomfort of lying half-curled on the couch, she slept well.

Adrian did not wake until well into the morning. When he did, he was surprised to see her there. 'I told you not to come today.'

'Did you?' She pretended innocence. 'What a nuisance I didn't hear you.'

He did not smile at her feeble joke. 'So you can go home.'

She humoured him as she would a plaintive child. 'Yes, soon, when you're better.'

His snort of irritation, muted though it was with weakness, gave her hope that he was beginning to improve. He took a little more food that day, and though his cough still tore at his body, by the evening he seemed more alert. She asked permission to tidy his clothes, and then his bedroom, and he said, 'Please yourself.'

So she folded his things in a neat pile and placed them on a chair, then she dusted his dressing-table and found a runner to cover the bare wood. She took the cleaner over the carpet and all the time she was working, she was conscious of his eyes watching her. 'If only he would start objecting to my tidying-up campaign,' she thought, 'then I'd know he was really improving.' But he just let her get on with it, and made no objection at all.

She stayed the night again in his living-room. About mid-morning, she went in to him and he was awake. He said, 'You here again? I can't get rid of you, can I?'

She laughed. 'Why, do you want to?'

'Frankly, yes.'

She laughed again, refusing to take him seriously, but he persisted, 'Why do you keep coming back? I honestly wish you wouldn't.'

She frowned. What was he trying to say? She shut her mind to the implications and left him. While he was sleeping, she went to the shops and bought some food to replenish his dwindling stocks. She hurried back, knowing the doctor would be calling, but she was too late. Mrs. Fields told her he had seen Adrian and gone already.

'What did he say, Mrs. Fields?'

'Oh, he's getting on nicely, dear. The illness is following its usual course.'

'He's not a very co-operative patient, Mrs. Fields.'

'What man is, dear? You'll learn that soon enough when you're married to him.'

He was sitting up when she went in. He sighed long-sufferingly. 'You really are like that gnat I once compared you with, aren't you? You keep on buzzing round me so much you'll soon drive me mad.'

'Then you'll have to swat me good and hard, won't you? Until you do, I'll just keep on buzzing. Now, is there anything you want?'

He paused before answering, and she saw a certain speculative gleam come into his eye as he looked her over which assured her beyond doubt that he was beginning to get better. But all he said was, 'Er – no, thanks. Not at present.'

'Want anything to read? Newspaper, magazine, or perhaps a textbook to polish up your maths?'

He smiled at this, as she had meant him to. 'Now there's impudence for you! Whoever heard of a cheeky gnat?'

He really was getting better. But towards evening, he flagged again. 'Thought it was too good to last,' he growled as she turned his pillows and tucked him in that night. 'This virus thing I've got must be the king of them all.'

Next day, he was querulous. His progress seemed to have been arrested, and his cough was troublesome. He eyed her sourly as she stood at his bedside. 'You get here earlier every day. You must be spending a fortune on bus fares.'

She didn't enlighten him that she had not been home since Saturday. 'I'll send you in my bill. It'll clean out your bank balance.'

But he was not amused. 'Well, you can go straight home again. I'm getting up later today.'

This alarmed her. 'No, you're not, Adrian. You're not fit enough. You don't know how ill you've been.'

'Oh, don't I? I should know, since I've been the one to suffer. I've also suffered your presence constantly, it seems, not for days but for years. I don't want you here, is that clear?'

She battled with her tears and won. 'We can't always get what we want, can we?'

He gave her a scathing look. 'Unfortunately, no.'

'Now, about food. What would you like for breakfast?

An egg?'

'Oh, if you want to cook me an egg, go ahead. Anything for some peace.'

What was the matter with him? She swallowed the lump in her throat and chided herself for selfishness. She had wanted him to show some of his usual life and vitality, and now he was doing so, she resented it. She made some toast, poached an egg and took them in to him. Then she left him.

'Where are you going?'

'To have my breakfast in the kitchen,' she told him. 'Why?'

'Didn't you have it before you left home?'

Something deep down inside her uttered an ominous warning. Do not tell him, it said, do not tell him where you have stayed for the past three nights. 'No, I – er – was in too much of a hurry to get back to you.'

As the day passed, he became increasingly irritable. He kept calling to her to bring him papers and books, and she waited on him continuously and uncomplainingly, without receiving a word of thanks. Still he kept her on her feet, and as he settled down later than usual, she was late getting to bed herself.

Just before she turned out his light, he remarked, 'You can go home now, and don't come back tomorrow. Do you hear?'

She did not answer. Instead she wished him good night and left him. When at last she crept between the sheets on the couch, she was almost too tired to sleep. But sleep she did, and heavily, because when she awoke at last, it was late. She dressed hastily and when she came out of the bathroom, she heard footsteps. They were coming from Adrian's bedroom. Surely he had not got up? She tapped on his door and went in.

CHAPTER SIX

HE was walking up and down the room in his dressing gown and stopped abruptly when he saw her. 'What are you doing here at this hour? Have you just arrived?'

'Well, I . . .'

'I thought I told you not to come back?'

'But, Adrian, I—' She knew then that she would have to tell him the truth and risk the consequences. 'I've been here all the time. I slept here.'

His anger hit her in the face. 'You *what*? Where did you sleep?'

'On the couch. I – I found some sheets and blankets. I couldn't leave you, Adrian. You were so ill.'

'But I wasn't that ill. See,' he lifted his hands, 'I'm up and about.'

'You don't know how ill you've been, Adrian. You were not fit enough to leave. I had to sleep here in case you needed anything in the night.'

His eyes narrowed and cynicism masked his features. 'Of course, I should have remembered. You're an old hand at staying the night, as Wallis Mason would no doubt testify.'

The insinuation in his words made her sick with anger. After all she had done for him, how could he talk to her like that? 'Are you trying to make me hate you, I wonder,' she said through teeth tight with fury, 'because you're very nearly succeeding!'

He went on as though she had not spoken. 'So you risked your reputation yet again—'

'Reputation?' She spat out the word. 'According to you, I haven't got one left to risk. And yours, I assure you, will go completely unscathed, because I shall tell everyone it was my suggestion and my choice. Anyway, who's to know I stayed?'

'My landlady, for a start.'

'But she knows you've been ill. It was she who . . .'

'Look, now you've discovered I'm not as bad as you thought, would – you – please – go?'

'But I must get your breakfast and tidy up . . .'

He was dangerously calm. 'I'm telling you to get out. Good grief, woman, do I have to throw you out? Have you no pride?'

'Yes, I've got pride, but I've also got compassion, and the one is stronger than the other.'

He drew himself in. 'There's only one way to deal with this – show you I mean business.' He thrust his fists into his dressing gown pockets and walked towards her menacingly. He stopped in front of her and held her gaze. 'Understand this, I'm a normal male. You, my sweet, are a very attractive young woman. If you don't get out of my bedroom while I'm still in control of the situation, and more important, of myself,' his hand came up and gripped her chin, 'I state categorically that I won't be held responsible for what may happen between us in the very near future.'

Still she stood her ground. She saw his white face, his tired eyes, and she could not leave him. His arms went round her, his mouth found hers, then his whole manner underwent a change. His cheek pressed against her hair and he seemed to be clinging to her as if trying to draw the life and strength from her body into his. He sagged against her.

'Oh, God, I'm sorry, Rosalie, I'm sorry.'

They stood holding each other for a long time, then she led him back to sit on his bed. He put his head into his hands.

She whispered, 'Do you still want me to go?'

'Yes. I still want you to go.'

Quietly, without another word, she left him. She tidied up the living-room, folded the bedding and collected her belongings. She went downstairs and knocked on Mrs. Fields' door.

'I'm going now,' Rosalie told her. 'Adrian doesn't want me to stay any longer. He says he's – he's fit now,' without warning a sob caught in her throat and she was crying, 'he – he won't let me stay, Mrs. Fields. He's told me to get out, he ...'

'My dear, come into the dining-room. Don't upset your-self like that. He doesn't know what he's saying, dear. It's the illness, you see. It gets 'em depressed so as they turn on the ones they love. He doesn't mean a thing he says. I heard him shouting at you, and I thought, oh goodness, what's he saying to her?'

'But he's not well, Mrs. Fields,' she sobbed, 'he still needs looking after.'

'Look, dear, the best thing you can do is get hold of his mother. I've got the phone number of their neighbour somewhere. I had to phone her the other night to tell her he wasn't well, and wouldn't be going up there this week. She offered to come down then, but he wouldn't hear of it.' She searched behind the clock on the mantelpiece. 'Here it is. It's next door but one to his mother and they have to go and fetch her.'

Rosalie wrote the number in her diary. 'There's his breakfast, Mrs. Fields. He hasn't had any yet.'

'Don't you worry, dear. I'll look after him till his mother gets here.' Rosalie stood up. 'And when he comes to his senses and realizes what he's done, and the things he said to you, he'll be ever so sorry, you mark my words. So don't fret, dear. I'll tell his mother how good you've been to him. Why, you look tired out yourself.'

'Where will his mother sleep, Mrs. Fields?'

'I'll put up my folding bed for her, dear. She'll be very comfortable.'

So with the landlady's soothing words ringing in her ears, Rosalie went home.

She lifted the receiver and dialled the operator. What would she be like, this woman whose photograph she had studied so often? Would she resent the interference of a young woman she had never even heard of, let alone met? Will she be patronizing, Rosalie wondered, or will she treat me as a pursuing female who ought to be sent pack-ing by her son at the earliest opportunity?

She asked for the telephone number written in her diary, and soon a voice with a broad northern accent answered. She explained to the man at the other end that she wanted to speak to a neighbour of his, and gave her name, and soon a quiet voice with a pleasant north country sound said, 'Mrs. Crayford speaking.'

'Oh, Mrs. Crayford, you won't know me, but my name is Rosalie Parham.'

'Yes, I have heard of you, my dear. You must be the young lady my son has mentioned in his letters.'

Rosalie's heart raced with pleasure. 'He has? Well, I'm sorry, Mrs. Crayford, but Adrian has been quite ill. I've been staying there looking after him and he's getting better now, but he still isn't fit enough to be left on his own.' She took a deep breath. 'I would have gone on looking after him, but he – he told me he didn't want me to.'

'I see, dear, so you would like me to come and take your place?'

Rosalie's voice was eager as she answered, 'Is that possible, Mrs. Crayford? Do you think you could? I haven't told him I've phoned you. He would only have said I mustn't.'

'I'm quite sure he would, my dear,' his mother laughed. 'Does his landlady know?'

'She gave me your phone number and says she can let you have a bed.'

Mrs. Crayford said, 'I'll get a few things together in a case and I'll be on my way. I shall have to get someone to take me to Darlington, and I'll get the first train south from there. It's a good service, so I should arrive at my son's place lateish tonight. Before you ring off, my dear, I feel I must thank you for all you've done for him. I don't suppose you've had a word of thanks out of him.'

How well she knew her own son, Rosalie thought, smiling, and how reassuring it was to have a chat with this very pleasant mother of his.

'I didn't do it for thanks, Mrs. Crayford. I did it because – because he was in need.'

'I quite understand, my dear. Good-bye now. Don't worry any more. I'll soon be on my way.'

Rosalie fretted the rest of the week away. She wondered all the time how Adrian was getting on. She did not like to telephone. After all, it was none of her business now. She had no claim on him, and he was under no obligation to keep in touch with her. He had told her in unmistakable words just what he thought of her. Now she knew that he had condemned her, as his colleagues had done, for her friendship with Wallis.

Her parents came home and she watched their eyebrows rise as she told them how she had spent her week's holiday. She returned to work feeling unrefreshed and depressed. Of course, Adrian was not back. Her father had received a message that the doctor advised at least another week's recuperation for him before he would be fit enough to resume work.

Wallis claimed her every day for lunch. She knew she had nothing more to lose by letting her name be coupled with his. On Thursday evening of the first week back, she was working in her bedroom when the telephone rang. She thought it must be Nichol, because she had not heard from him since before half-term. He would of course have thought she was away.

But it wasn't Nichol. 'Rosalie?' Her heart bumped. 'Adrian here.'

'Hallo, Adrian.' Her voice sounded hoarse and she could hardly get the words out. 'How are you?'

'Much better, thanks. I was wondering if I might come and see you for a short time this evening.'

She heard joyful bells all around her. 'Of course, Adrian, I'd be glad to see you.'

'I'll be round in, say, fifteen minutes.'

She rang off. Soon his car swung into the driveway, and Rosalie had to stop herself from running to the front door to open it before he pressed the bell. The door chimes sounded joyously, and they stood there, looking at each other, motionless, for what seemed an eternity. Then, with a gentle smile, 'May I come in, Rosalie, or do I have to deliver my speech on the doorstep?'

'Oh, forgive me, Adrian. It's just that it's so good to see you back to normal.'

Her mother appeared at the study door. 'Adrian, how nice to see you again! You've had a wretched time, I hear.' She took his hand and called, 'Franklyn, Adrian's come!'

Franklyn welcomed him and assumed he would be joining them in the study. Adrian looked embarrassed and raised his eyebrows at Rosalie in silent inquiry, as if waiting for her to take action. 'Adrian wants to see me for a few minutes first, Dad.'

'Oh, go ahead, my boy. I'm so sorry. Tactless of me. We'll see you later, perhaps?' They disappeared into the study.

'Upstairs or down, Adrian?'

'Upstairs, Rosalie.'

In her bedroom, she told him, 'Sit down, Adrian. You look a lot better.'

Adrian sat in the armchair and she stood in front of him. 'I feel it, Rosalie, mainly thanks to you. I've come to—'

'To thank me for all I've done and apologize.' She sat on the arm of his chair and put her finger on his lips. 'Well, don't, Adrian. I don't want either.'

He caught her hand and put it to his cheek. 'Mrs. Fields told me I made you cry. I must apologize for that, at least.'

She drew her hand away gently. 'Well, let's leave it at that, Adrian.'

He stood and put his hands on her shoulders. 'Let's take it from there, you mean.'

He pulled her towards him, but she resisted and raised an expressionless face to his. 'There's nothing to take, Adrian. We can't ever be the strangers we once were, for obvious reasons. But it's plain to me that we can never be anything more to each other, because even friendship requires trust, and you have no trust in me.' She felt as though the words she spoke were lynching her soul. Slowly but surely she was tearing herself apart, but she had to go on. 'I know what you think now about my behaviour and my morals . . .'

'Rosalie,' he sounded desperate, 'I retract all I said.

Every single word.'

She moved out of his reach and shook her head. 'You don't, you know. You really believe I'm Wallis Mason's property.'

He made a sharp movement towards her, as if to silence her.

'Those words I spoke, and which I now so bitterly regret, were spoken under the stress of the circumstances.'

Again she shook her head. 'You really believe it, Adrian, deep inside you. Your guard was down, because you were too fatigued to pay lip service to the restraining barriers of politeness, and you spoke from your heart, from your deepest conviction.'

'But, Rosalie, hear me, at least . . .'

Relentlessly, she carried on, because she had to. She raised her head in a kind of desperate pride. 'And when I tell you that tomorrow evening I'm going home with him to see Melanie, and on Saturday we're taking her to the local theatre to see a children's matinée, and I'm spending part of the evening there afterwards, you'll put the same construction on it as all the others, and the trust that you're so desperately trying to invest in me will die a quick, painless death.' Like my heart at this moment, she whispered to herself, as she watched his face harden into a mask.

His lips were tight. He sat down as if his legs had not sufficient strength to support him. 'Are you trying to drive me away?'

She did not answer and there was a painful silence. Then she asked, 'Has your mother gone home?'

'Yes, this morning. She wanted to meet you, but I . . .'

She turned on him then. The person he knew she was longing to meet had wanted to meet her, yet he had refused to allow the meeting. 'No, you wouldn't let her contaminate herself. You wouldn't let her meet someone with such low moral standards as I've got, who runs around with a married man, who pretends she's his wife. . . .' She turned away, unable to stop the tears. 'You're no better than the others,' she sobbed, 'your accusations have

113

no foundation, your judgment is based on false evidence, and no matter how much I might declare my innocence, you won't believe me. You won't even listen.'

He stood behind her, lowered his hands to her shoulders. He whispered, 'Stop associating with him, Rosalie, that's all I ask.'

'I can't, because of Melanie.'

'You're putting your head in a noose, and he will tighten it and tighten it until,' his fingers gripped her neck, 'he's got you like that. Believe me, Rosalie, I know. We've seen it all before. You're not the first by any means. The difference with you is that he's had to play it your way, to use his child to lure you into his web, because he knew he wouldn't get you any other way.' He turned her round and looked deep and urgently into her eyes. 'Do as I ask, Rosalie. Once more, I ask you, plead with you, for your own sake, if no one else's, stop associating with him.'

A child's appealing face and clinging hands burned an image on her brain and she shook her head helplessly. 'I can't, Adrian, because of Melanie.'

He pushed her away from him and walked to the door. 'Good night, Rosalie. Good-bye.'

With that one word, she knew he had shut her out of his life for ever.

Wallis was becoming more possessive as the days passed. He was openly displaying his feelings towards her, and as they walked along the corridor at lunch-time, he would put his arm round her and when she tried to move away, he would grip her so that she could not escape. When they left the staff restaurant after their meal, he would hold her round the waist. At other times, he would call her into his room, pretending he wanted to discuss her work, then he would kiss her. The more she resisted, the more determined he became.

'Stop playing hard to get, Miss Puritan,' he murmured in her ear on one occasion. 'I know your kind. You only do it to provoke.'

When she protested, he told her, 'I'm desperately in

love with you, darling. Can't you read the signs?'

But she couldn't break away because of Melanie. The child clung closer every time she went to see her, and every time she left, Melanie cried just a little more. She was racked with doubt and uncertainty, but always, Melanie's need of her conquered.

Wallis was not oblivious to Rosalie's struggle. He watched her sometimes with his daughter as though he were secretly enjoying it, knowing that things were slowly but surely going his way.

Adrian seemed to have cut her out of his life. When they met, he barely acknowledged her. When he came to the house, she kept out of his way, and he out of hers. One evening they misjudged each other's movements and collided in the hall. They both apologized immediately, but the contact of their bodies caused such a surge of longing within her that she lifted her eyes to his, and with them pleaded for his forgiveness. She saw his look of steel and recoiled as he deliberately raised his hands to put her out of his way.

The end of the term was approaching, and her father told her one day, 'Adrian's coming to a meal tomorrow evening, Rosalie, and he's bringing Jane with him. So there'll be two extra to cater for. Can you manage that?'

Her heart sank, but she told him she could. She wished she did not have to join them, and tried to think of ways of getting out of it, but knew she would have to be there to carry out her usual jobs of cook, waitress and kitchen maid.

Jane was in a gay mood the following evening. Her pretty face seemed to hold an extra sparkle these days, and Rosalie noted with gloom the attentive way Adrian looked after her needs. She praised the cook expansively, turning to Sarah, who directed her attention to Rosalie with a wave of her hand.

'Thank our offspring, Jane,' she commented airily. 'She's the housekeeper and general provider in this family. She's so good at it, I let her get on with it.'

Franklyn whispered loudly, behind his hand, 'Confidentially, we do believe she must have studied it as part of her degree course – the more practical, useful part of her degree course!'

'Implying, you will notice,' Rosalie countered bitterly, 'that the subjects I really did study were useless – strictly non-scientific, therefore useless.'

They all laughed, except Adrian, and his dark eyes rested on her reflectively.

He smiled slightly and said, in a curious tone, 'I attended one of your daughter's lectures recently, Franklyn.' As he spoke, he spread out his paper serviette on the table cloth and folded it into a neat, precise triangle. Then he put it aside and leaned back in his chair. 'She was sitting on the floor, on an inflated cushion, surrounded by students who were doing likewise.'

There was a burst of laughter from the others and Rosalie seized her serviette and crumpled it viciously into a tight, white ball. Then she looked at Adrian as if she would like to stuff it down his throat.

He smiled at her action and his eyes played over her face. 'I listened to her lecture, perforce, because I was inspecting, at her request, some electrical equipment which had gone wrong. After an interesting introduction of the subject matter by the lady lecturer in question, there followed a discussion so informative and enlightening, I nearly asked permission to join in myself.' He held Rosalie's astonished gaze. 'I state categorically, here and now, that I retract without reserve all the derogatory and denigrating statements I have made in the past about General Studies, which she teaches, and about the subjects she took in her degree.' She flushed with pleasure, she couldn't help it, especially when he added, with obvious sincerity, 'Any time she requires a reference as to her teaching ability, I should be only too delighted to oblige.'

Again there was laughter, but this time there was a subtle and pleasing difference about it. 'Well, well,' said Franklyn.

'It seems we have a clever daughter, Franklyn,' Sarah

said.

Jane laughed, 'Now isn't that nice?'

'And the ugly duckling turned into a beautiful swan before their very eyes.' Rosalie really meant it as a joke, but it came out strongly laced with cynicism, and she could have bitten out her tongue as she watched the warmth in Adrian's eyes grow cold.

She was desperate to divert attention from herself, so she began to clear away the dishes, and the others drifted into the study. 'Leave those,' her mother said, as usual, 'I'll do them later.'

When they had gone, Rosalie started on the washing-up. She was half-way through when Adrian came in, took a towel and began to dry the dishes. Not a word was spoken and her irritation was growing, quite irrationally, with every passing minute. How could he stand so close, yet treat her as if she were invisible? What right had he got to condemn her, as though she had contravened every moral law in the book? At last she turned on him, her voice choked with passion.

'There's no need to help me, no need at all. Why you always think I welcome your help, I fail to understand. Go back to your girl-friend. She needs you more than I do.'

He drew in his lips. 'I seem to remember your saying that once before, and I was fool enough not to take the hint. This time I will.' He flung the tea towel on to the table. 'I'm damned if I'm going to stand here and be insulted whenever I try, out of sheer kindness of heart — nothing else — to relieve you of some of your work.' He went to the door.

'Thank you so much for your help,' she flung at his rigid back, and to her intense annoyance, her voice cracked as she continued sarcastically, 'which was so willingly and so pleasantly given!'

He paused in the doorway and she changed her tone saying softly, 'Thank you for coming over to the enemy camp at dinner.' Her voice wavered dangerously, but she went on, 'I appreciated your gesture, although I know you didn't mean a word you said.' He turned at that, and there was an odd look in his eyes. He seemed about to speak, but perceptibly hardened himself and returned to the study.

Some time later, Nichol phoned. 'Hallo, darling,' he said, quite unabashed. 'Long time no see.'

'Good heavens,' Rosalie joked. 'A voice from the distant past!'

'I'm so sorry, Rosalie, but I've been busy.'

'I quite understand, Nichol. She's very pretty.'

There was an embarrassed pause, then, 'Who?'

'Jane Halewood, your new girl-friend. Who else?'

'Jane? She's not my girl-friend. She won't—'

'Oh, I see. She's being unco-operative and you're not making any headway? Well, why not come round this evening? She's here working, but no doubt we can arrange to let you see her over coffee.'

'Is she really at your house, Rosalie? You don't mind, then, if I . . .'

'I wouldn't have invited you if I did mind, would I? But be prepared for a struggle. You've got a rival – her other boy-friend, Dr. Adrian Crayford.'

'What, him?' he said, in an 'I'll soon fix him' tone of voice. 'I'll be round in, say, ten minutes. All right?' He rang off.

Ten minutes later, he was on the doorstep. He seized Rosalie and attempted to kiss her, but she resisted. 'Don't let's be hypocritical about it, Nichol. It's all over between us, isn't it? If there ever was anything.'

He was about to protest, when the study door opened. 'Who's that?' Franklyn asked, and saw for himself. He withdrew his head after a perfunctory 'good evening'. He obviously told the others who it was, because Jane's voice trilled with delighted surprise. Nichol heard it and responded as though it were a love-call from a distant forest. 'That's Jane's voice,' he breathed, with a seraphic smile.

'My word,' Rosalie thought, 'you've got it badly!'

They sat in the lounge. 'Anyway,' Nichol said, as though their conversation had never been interrupted, 'I heard that you were having – er – a busy time yourself.

Much in demand and all that by a certain person who shall be nameless – simply because propriety dictates it, of course.'

'What you really mean is, that you've heard from Jane that I've been running round with a married man.'

He looked acutely uncomfortable. 'Well, I wouldn't put it as bluntly as that—'

'There's no need. I've done it for you.'

'Rosalie darling, why are you so bitter these days? I haven't condemned you.'

'Not out loud, but silently, like everyone else.'

'If you don't like what people are saying, why don't you break away – or is it too far gone for that?'

Her eyes flashed dangerously. 'I don't know what you mean. If you want to know, it's for his young daughter's sake I'm doing it.'

Nichol cleared his throat noisily. 'H'm, yes, well, it sounds a good story, plausible and all that . . .'

'Look, Nichol, I invited you here out of the kindness of my heart, to see a girl you seem to like very much. But if I'm going to have insinuations thrown my way, and nasty hints based solely on rumours—'

'Sorry, darling. Forgive me. I'll be a good boy.' He moved beside her on the couch and took her hand. The door opened and Adrian came in. Nichol's eyes searched in the background and were rewarded with a sight of the vision which apparently haunted his dreams.

'Sorry to interrupt,' Adrian said dryly, 'but you have company, whether you want it or not.'

He watched with evident surprise at the way Nichol dropped Rosalie's hand as though it had the properties of a piece of burning coal. Jane appeared in the doorway and Nichol rose to gaze at her with unashamed delight. 'Jane,' he murmured, 'what a lovely surprise!'

'Hardly that,' Rosalie could not resist saying, 'since I told you she was here and invited you to see her.'

Adrian's eyebrows rose in cynical, silent comment.

'Is that true, Nichol?' Jane smiled at him. 'Did you know I was here and that's why you came?'

Adrian appeared to be wounded to the heart. 'What, Jane, deserting me for another man, when our friendship has just begun to blossom?'.

Rosalie stood abruptly and went to make the coffee. As she reached the door and turned to shut it, she caught the remains of a taunting grin which Adrian had flung at her. She slammed the door.

If the crockery cracked as a result of her clattering them into position on the tray, she did not care. She felt as though she had to break something or crack inside herself. When Adrian came in, she almost picked up a cup and threw it in his face. He leaned carelessly against the wall and watched. 'What's the matter, can't you bear to take a back seat and be outshone by another woman?' he jeered.

Her look should have frozen him to the marrow, but it did not even chill him. 'I can't bear to see two grown men,' she ground out, 'make complete asses of themselves over a simpering girl, that's all!'

Her hands were shaking, but she could not do anything about it. She could not seem to control them any more. Adrian came across and held them. 'Calm down, girl. Take a hold on yourself.'

His touch stung her like a live wire and she dragged her hands from his. 'You're as bad as he is. I'm not coming in there again, so you've got a clear field. Those three cups are for the lounge, these two I'll take to my parents in the study. I'll take my coffee upstairs to my room, and have it in peace and quiet. And blessed solitude.'

She lifted the smaller tray and went to the door. 'And you can tell my boy-friend — correction, ex-boy-friend — that he needn't bother to say good night to me. He can spend his time instead taking his new girl-friend home.' She turned on the sarcasm. 'Unless of course you want that pleasure yourself, in which case you'll just have to fight it out with him, won't you?'

He gave an infuriating smile and carried the other tray into the lounge.

Later, Rosalie heard Jane leaving. A car started up and

drove away. She wondered dully and without much interest who had won the battle to take her home. Then Adrian laughed downstairs in the study, and with a lift of the heart, she discovered the answer.

CHAPTER SEVEN

A few evenings later, Rosalie finished her college work early and decided to wash her hair. She set it and dried it and it swung, soft and shining, round her neck and down to her shoulders. Then she put on her oldest trousers, bright red ones with a patch on one knee and a hole in the other, and wore an emerald green blouse with one or two buttons missing. She felt an urge to do some dress-making.

She unwrapped a piece of floral dress fabric she had recently bought in a sale and spread it on the floor, placed a paper pattern on top of it and pinned it here and there. Then she proceeded to cut round it. She was on her knees, stretched across the material and still cutting, when she heard footsteps mounting the stairs, followed by a tap at the door. She called 'Come in, Dad,' and continued snipping round the pattern.

'Is there no end to your accomplishments, Miss Parham?'

'Adrian!' She quivered at the sound of his voice and sat back on her heels, frowning. 'What do you want?'

'You know,' he commented with a crooked smile, 'you really should write "welcome" on the mat, because it's a word you don't seem to have in your vocabulary these days.'

'I'm so sorry.' She hoped her sarcasm would shrivel him up, but it only seemed to amuse him. 'Next time you come, I'll salaam. Would that make you any happier?'

'Much.' He crouched beside her and she wished he would go away. He indicated the material and the pattern lying on it. 'This reveals you've got a technical mind. Explain it to me, will you?'

She tried to put derision into her answering grin. 'Explain it to *you*? You simply wouldn't comprehend, Dr. Crayford. I could no more teach you the intricacies and technicalities of dressmaking than you could teach me the mysteries of mathematics.'

'There's no mystery about mathematics. You were obviously frightened off the subject at school by bad teaching, given by teachers who couldn't make you understand it because they probably couldn't understand it themselves.' His eyes assessed her, and she looked down in confusion. 'Anyway, I could teach you maths even if I were blindfolded and handcuffed.'

'Oh?' she challenged. 'What makes you so sure?'

'In the first place, you have the necessary intelligence, and secondly,' his eyes dropped from her face and proceeded on a voyage of discovery over the rest of her, 'you'd be such fertile material to work on.' He straightened himself and drawled, with a mocking smile, 'So – er – malleable, so pliable.'

She flushed and stood up and was dismayed to find that her blouse had come adrift from the waistband of her slacks and that her bare midriff was showing. She tucked it in with some embarrassment, while he watched, smiling, and she asked him irritably what he wanted.

'Unfortunately, we haven't a typist this evening. Jane couldn't come and there's some important stuff waiting to be typed. Your father tells me you have that ability, amongst your many others, so could we persuade you to help us out?'

She said, uncertainly, 'I'm not a very good typist.'

'That wouldn't matter. What we want is to get some handwritten notes into a form legible enough to be worked on, and the only way to do that is to type them. You could do that, surely?'

'Probably. Well, all right. . . .'

He patted her arm. 'There's a nice, obliging girl. Come along then, into the lion's den.'

'Oh, but,' she looked down at herself, 'I can't come in these things. I must change.'

'Why? There's only your parents – and you wouldn't consider me worth changing for, now would you? Anyway,' he narrowed his eyes as he looked her up and down, 'I find myself agreeing with the poet, Robert Herrick, wasn't it? – who found "a sweet disorder in the dress" rather – er – bewitching.' He looked at his watch. 'That apart, there isn't time, so come along.'

Her father told Adrian to explain everything, and left them to it. She sat down at the typewriter, wishing her father had stayed. She did not want to be alone with Adrian, especially as he was bending over her, so near that she wondered if he was doing it on purpose. She tried to steady her heart-beats as he murmured, 'You have a sweet scent about you. What perfume do you use?'

'It's probably the shampoo I washed my hair with.'

'Oh, I see. I thought it looked very soft and fetching this evening.'

She changed the subject quickly, and at last he left her to get on with the work. He sat quietly in an armchair writing in a notebook, and whenever she needed help, he came across and stood next to her and gave precise and lucid explanations.

By the time her father returned, Rosalie had finished typing all the notes. He thanked her twice over, looked from her to Adrian and said he would go and help Sarah with the coffee.

Rosalie got up and stretched, then roamed round the room, looking out of the window, rearranging some flowers which needed no rearranging, and tidied books in the bookshelves which were already tidy. All the time, Adrian was sitting relaxed in an armchair, reading.

He looked up and said, 'You're very restless, Miss Parham. Objecting to being closeted in solitary confinement with me?'

'Not half as much as you must be objecting to being alone with me, Dr. Crayford.'

He extended his legs lazily, and reclined in the chair, hands in his pockets. His book fell to the floor, but he ignored it.

'If you don't like the *status quo* between us, you know what to do to remedy it, don't you? Or,' he drawled, 'has Mason already taken you beyond the point of no return?'

'That's no business of yours. I refuse to satisfy your morbid curiosity by giving you an answer to that – that impertinent question.'

'It's all right,' he closed his eyes, 'I already know the answer to it, my sweet, without your telling me.'

'Oh?' She wheeled round. 'What is the answer, then? And how can you be sure you know it?'

'Ah,' his eyes fluttered open, 'now you're asking. And I'm not telling.'

His knowing smile tantalized her, but she was refused the chance of pressing her question because her parents came in with the coffee. They talked about the end-of-term dance. 'We've bought tickets,' Franklyn said. 'Are you going, Rosalie?'

'Yes. As far as I know, Nichol is coming with me – that is,' she looked at Adrian, 'if you're still taking Jane?'

'As far as I know, I am. She knows I don't dance. If she's all that anxious to dance herself,' he grinned, 'we could always swop partners.'

'You seem to forget I like dancing, too.'

'Oh, yes. Something not to be missed, Nichol said. You almost tempt me to learn, just for the experience of partnering you.'

Her parents laughed. 'You needn't worry. Rosalie is never at a loss for partners at a dance. We've never known her be a wallflower yet.'

Adrian frowned, drained his cup, said a brief good night and went home.

Rosalie was going to tea with Wallis and Melanie. Her parents were going out for the evening, so there was no meal to cook. She tapped on Wallis's door and went in. He rose, held out his hand and she went to him. He swept her into his arms and kissed her, just as he always did. She had long ago given up trying to resist, because it seemed to make him more persistent, but she found his possessive embraces increasingly difficult to tolerate.

They walked out of the building together; his arm was round her, and Adrian overtook them, passing by as if they had never met before. Unluckily, his car was parked next to Wallis's, and his eyes coldly avoided them as he drove away.

As usual, Rosalie found her way to Wallis's kitchen. She knew it now almost as well as she knew her mother's. She set the table while Wallis went next door to get his daughter. They had their tea, and Rosalie tried her hardest to be cheerful and meet Melanie's gay mood.

Wallis helped with the washing-up. He said with a sly smile, 'Quite one of the family now, aren't you, Rosalie? With a little stretch of my imagination, I might almost regard you as my wife.'

She repulsed the repugnance his words awoke inside her, and smiled. 'Not by any stretch of my imagination could I look upon you as my husband.'

She was unprepared for the ugly look which swept across his face, but it was muted, almost as soon as it came, into a distorted grin. 'Marriage doesn't enter my thoughts, darling. It doesn't have to, you know.'

She dried her hands on the towel. 'I'll go and play with Melanie for a while, before she goes to bed.'

He let her go without comment. It was usually Melanie's happiest hour. She had Rosalie to herself, and she indulged the child's every whim. They played 'schools' and 'shops', they spring-cleaned the dolls' house and put the 'babies' to bed. They read stories and made them up. Rosalie bathed her and dried her and took her back to her room, then Melanie put her arms round Rosalie's neck.

'I wish you were my mummy,' she sighed into her hair. 'Why aren't you ever here in the morning when I wake up?'

'That's just what I'd like to know, Melanie,' her father said, standing in the doorway.

Rosalie ignored him. 'But, Melanie darling, I'm not your mummy and never will be. You must, you *must* understand that.'

'Don't go, Rosalie. Stay with me.' She clung tighter.

'I'm going to my own home quite soon after you've settled down, young lady, and you know it, don't you?'

'Yes, I know it, and that's why I want you to stay, and you could give me my breakfast in the morning. So don't go, Rosalie.' Tears began to dampen Rosalie's hair, and she tried to disentangle herself from Melanie's arms, but the more she tried, the more they clung.

Rosalie panicked. 'You *must* let me go, Melanie.' Her voice was sharper than she had intended and Melanie began to howl. 'Why doesn't Wallis help me?' Rosalie asked herself desperately, but knew she would get no assistance from him. He was, after all, watching his carefully nurtured plans come to fruition.

She freed herself at last, but Melanie clamped on to her shoulders and was crying hysterically. She felt trapped. She looked up and saw Wallis's sharp, elongated features, his large pointed nose, the way his reddish hair sprang short and wiry from his head. She noticed his small, watchful eyes fixed on her with a predatory, unwavering stare.

He made a swift pouncing movement and fastened his fingers round his daughter's waist. Rosalie cowered involuntarily.

'Poor little rabbit,' he said, addressing his daughter, but fixing his calculating, waiting gaze on Rosalie's frightened face.

He tugged Melanie away and shook her. 'Stop it, child. Stop that noise!' Slowly the sobs diminished, and Rosalie reached out for the hopeless little form, drawing her close and comforting her.

'I want my mummy back,' she whispered. 'When will she come?'

'Ask your daddy, darling,' Rosalie murmured. 'I don't suppose it will be long now.'

She led the child to bed, tucked her in and kissed her. 'I'll stay until you sleep,' Rosalie promised. 'I won't leave you till then.'

She soon relaxed and slept, and Rosalie crept from the room and closed the door softly. Wallis was in the lounge, drinking. 'I'm going home,' she told him firmly.

'But, darling,' he put down his glass and came to her side, 'at least have a drink with me.'

'I'm sorry, Wallis. I must go. Now.'

He tried to kiss her, but she evaded him, knowing what a dangerous game she was playing. He tried making love to her, but she pulled away and went to the door. 'If you don't take me, I'll get a bus. I'm determined to go.'

'I could lock the door, sweetie.' He smiled unpleasantly. 'Then you really would be caught, wouldn't you?'

Swiftly she grabbed her jacket and handbag and was out in the driveway before he was aware of her intention. 'Good-bye, Wallis,' she called, and walked to the gate, but he caught her up.

'But, darling, of course I'll take you home. Don't be scared of me. I wouldn't harm a hair of your beautiful head.'

She got into the car and they drove in silence to the end of her road. 'You'll come again soon, Rosalie? You know I wouldn't really go against your wishes – ever, don't you?'

His tone was soft and coaxing, and his anxiety appeared to be genuine, even to Rosalie's suspicious eyes, but she hesitated. 'Perhaps,' was all she would say.

She let herself into the house. She had hoped to be alone, but was shocked to find that Adrian was there. She remembered her parents had had another key cut for his use. He must have parked his car along the road and she had missed it.

She recoiled from the coldness in his eyes as he walked along the hall from the kitchen to the study. She knew he must have seen how tired she was. She felt overwrought and dejected and longed for his comfort. But he shut the study door in her face.

She rushed upstairs and threw herself on the bed, abandoning herself to tears. She had to cry, she had to give freedom to this great gushing force of emotion which had built up into a swirling river inside her. As the tears gathered and fell, like a great waterfall hurling on to the rocks below, she found an incalculable release from the tension which had accumulated in her body over the past months.

At last she grew quiet and became aware of the murmur of voices in the hall below. Then she heard footsteps and a gentle knock. 'Rosalie, darling?' Her mother's voice roused her.

'Yes?'

'May I come in, darling?'

'All right.' She gripped her tear-soaked handkerchief and unlocked the door. 'Hallo, Mum. I'm sorry I'm not very presentable.' She sat on the bed.

'So Adrian was right. He said he heard you crying. Is there anything I can do to help you, darling? You look so distressed.'

She lifted heavy eyes and looked at her mother's slim figure standing in front of her. She wanted to say, 'Hold me, like I do Melanie, comfort me, like I do Melanie. I'm really a small girl lost in a bewildering problem world. I want you to tell me everything will be all right, like I do Melanie.'

She saw her mother's arms hanging loosely at her sides, saw the puzzled frown, sensed her hesitation and uncertainty. Rosalie opened her mouth to speak, to pour it all out, to implore, 'Tell me what to do for the best.'

But she said, shaking her head, 'It's really too complicated to explain.'

'Can't you try?'

She shrugged hopelessly.

'Has – has something happened that – that you're regretting, Rosalie?'

She gave a tearful smile. 'No, Mum. I know what you mean. You don't have to worry on that score.'

Her mother looked relieved, but went on, 'Your father says he's been worried about you lately. He's seen you with—'

'I know what you're going to say. You can tell Dad neither he nor you need share the views of apparently every other member of staff at the college.'

'What is it that's troubling you so, then?'

Rosalie stared into space. It was no good, she simply could not communicate with this mother of hers.

'Darling,' Sarah said plaintively, 'you know I love you, don't you? I'm sorry if I don't understand. I feel so inadequate. I know I'm not a very good mother. I do my best, but ...'

'Oh, Mum.' Rosalie stood and put her arms round her

mother, cuddled and comforted her, 'Don't say that!' Tears stole into her eyes, tears of a different, sadder sort, that this brilliant and accomplished woman was so conscious of her inadequacies and imperfections as a parent that she felt a failure. Rosalie knew then that in experience and insight she was older and wiser than her mother and infinitely better equipped to deal with the rough and tumble of the world outside. At last they understood each other, and felt closer than they had ever done before.

Rosalie was dressing for the dinner-dance and she was in a desperate and reckless mood. None of her problems had been solved, but for one evening she was determined to forget them. She looked in the mirror and saw a stranger there, a stranger in a tight-fitting black dress, low-cut, sleeveless, with sparkling silver thread interwoven into the fabric to bring it to startling life.

Adrian would notice her, that was clear. She could not escape notice in such a dress. She combed her hair into a soft, sweeping style round her face, slipped into black evening sandals and picked up her black satin handbag. Her face was pale, despite the make-up which she had applied liberally. Her eyes lacked lustre, but burned with defiance.

Nichol was calling for her and when the door chimes sounded she went down to let him in. Her parents had already left. Nichol stood in the hall and gave a prolonged wolf whistle.

'You'll be a sensation in that, Rosalie.' He put his arm round her, but she pulled away.

'You can save that for Jane.'

'But, darling, in that dress, you ask for it. You can't invite a man with one hand, and hold him off with the other.'

'Shall we go, Nichol? There's sherry before the meal. We don't want to miss that.'

Guests were assembled in the college hall, and tables had been set aside for the serving of drinks. When Nichol took Rosalie's hand and led her through the swing doors, eyes opened wider. As she sipped her sherry and talked to

Nichol, she looked round the hall and found Adrian. He was deep in conversation with Jane, who was gazing into his eyes with the childlike expression she had made her own. Her pale blue filmy dress emphasized the fairness of her skin, and her short blonde hair curled round her cheeks. Then Adrian turned and saw Rosalie.

The shocked animosity in his eyes made her even more defiant. She turned back to Nichol and joked about the effect the sherry was having on her appetite and her sense of balance, and laughed with what she hoped was abandoned gaiety. Their laughter attracted some attention and Rosalie noticed Wallis standing alone, watching them intently. He seemed to be trying to assess their relationship.

Nichol played up to her. 'There's something about you tonight, darling, that's absolutely devastating. I won't leave your side, in case I lose you.'

'You're not my boy-friend now, Nichol. Look round the room at all the unattached females. You're free to take your pick as far as I'm concerned.'

'Don't make your brush-off so darned obvious, darling.' He put his hand on her bare arm. 'And the more you push me away, the more I'll cling.'

She turned to find Adrian watching her, and the smile which she directed at him was full of a gaiety she did not feel. He gave no answering smile. Nichol followed her eyes. 'Look, isn't that Jane standing with Adrian? I'm going over there. Coming?'

Rosalie followed reluctantly.

'Jane!' Nichol enthused. 'How charming you look.'

'Thank you, kind Nichol.' She gave him a sweeping curtsy. 'Hallo, Rosalie.' She blinked affectedly. 'What have you done to yourself? You look like a sophisticated twin sister, not like you at all.' She turned to her partner. 'Don't you agree?'

Adrian made no comment with his lips, but his eyes made a prolonged and acid speech. They conveyed the unmistakable message that if circumstances had allowed, he would have removed the dress from her body as forcibly as he had taken the cigarette packet from her hand that afternoon at his flat.

'I rather thought I'd cause a certain amount of – er – agitation in certain quarters.' She smiled sweetly at Jane then swept her eyes round to Adrian, who looked away.

Jane, conformist from top to toe, was aghast. 'You mean you did it on purpose?'

'Could be.' She smiled enigmatically. 'I have to live up to my notorious reputation. I couldn't let the rumour-mongers down.' She saw her parents. 'Excuse me.'

They were standing with a group of people across the room, and her father saw her first. 'Rosalie, dear.' Then he saw her dress. 'I can't say I've seen you in that before, my dear.' He touched his wife's hand. 'Have you, Sarah?'

She frowned. 'Darling, why – I mean, when did you buy that?'

'Oh, recently. Don't you like it? I thought it rather effective.'

'It's effective all right, darling, but – well, it's your choice. Where's Adrian? Oh, he's over there, with Jane.' She waved.

Someone shouted, 'Dinner is served!' Rosalie moved to Nichol's side. He turned gallant and bowed and held out his arm. They followed close behind Adrian and Jane, and climbed the three flights of stairs to the refectory, where the tables had been pushed together and set at right angles to each other.

'Our seats, Rosalie.' Nichol pointed to cards bearing their names. 'Look who's opposite – Jane and Adrian.'

Rosalie had to suppress her annoyance. Why did they have to be placed opposite these two? She did not want to sit for an hour watching Jane simpering all over Adrian. She looked round furtively for Wallis, and was relieved to see that he was at the other end of the room. Dinner was served by a firm of private caterers and proceeded at the usual slow pace. Nichol insisted on buying a bottle of wine for the four of them.

Rosalie could not understand why, but as the meal progressed, she felt increasingly apprehensive and haunted by an elusive anxiety. She sensed that someone was watching her, and her eyes were involuntarily drawn to the other end of the room. As she looked, Wallis removed his eyes from her.

She caught at Nichol's arm a little wildly, seeking the comfort of his familiar person. Adrian watched and raised his eyebrows. Nichol was surprised and patted her hand. 'Hallo, darling,' he said, as though he was seeing her for the first time. 'Anything wrong?'

She withdrew her hand quickly. 'Sorry, Nichol.'

'Oh, don't apologize, darling. You're so darned attractive tonight, I can hardly refuse you anything.' But he said it with a broad smile and a wink at Jane.

When dinner was over, they made their way down the stairs to the main hall. On the stage the five-piece band had got itself organized, and as soon as the beat of the music began, Nichol led Rosalie on to the floor. Adrian and Jane were sitting in a corner talking. Adrian's arm was round the back of Jane's chair and Rosalie knew they were watching her and Nichol as they moved round the room together.

'You're a delight to dance with,' Nichol murmured, nuzzling his cheek against her hair.

'Don't get affectionate, Nichol. We're only friends now, not sweethearts. Unless, of course, you want to make Jane jealous, in which case, carry on.'

Nichol looked shocked. Then he made a face as though he had tasted lemon juice. 'You're too sour to be true this evening, darling. Sweeten up a bit, or I shall make a bee-line for Jane.'

'By all means, Nichol. I'll soon find another partner.'

She saw his lips tighten. When the music ended, he led her across to the other two, bowed formally in front of Jane, and held out his hand. Jane rose and accompanied him graciously to the dance floor. Rosalie stood alone, watching them, fighting off a lost, vulnerable feeling.

'Sit down, Rosalie.' Adrian's irritated voice cut across her thoughts. She ignored him, then saw Wallis making his devious way in her direction. She sat down at once.

'Adrian,' she smiled sweetly at him and said the first thing that came into her head, 'I wish you could dance.'

He raised his eyebrows laconically. 'Oh? And what makes you think I'd want to dance with you?'

She hardly heard him. He followed her eyes and saw the reason for her agitation. He smiled maliciously. 'It looks as though you're about to get yourself a partner anyway. An old friend of yours is stalking you.'

'Adrian, please, I . . .'

He stood up. 'He's all yours,' he said nonchalantly, and walked away.

Rosalie jumped up and followed him, pushed past him and sought shelter with her parents who were sitting at the back of the hall. They smiled and made room for her, and went on with their conversation. Soon a member of the General Studies staff approached and asked her to dance. From that moment on, she hardly sat down. She swayed and twisted with the younger set, danced in the conventional manner with others, and did everything in her power to keep out of the way of Wallis Mason.

And all the time he kept on her tracks, never letting up, getting progressively nearer.

Nichol claimed her once or twice, when he could tear himself away from Jane. She was conscious of Adrian watching her most of the time, because, against her will, she kept seeking him out. He was sitting with her parents and she longed to join them, but knew that if she had done so, Adrian would have moved away.

Her partner left her, and in the pause before someone else claimed her, she saw Adrian leave the hall. She fought off a feeling of dismay. Was he going home? Surely he would not leave Jane unattended like that? After all, she was really his partner, not Nichol's, and he would have to take her home.

'*Caught you at last, Rosalie!*' A hand gripped her arm and she swung round and stared into Wallis Mason's grinning face. 'Come with me, I'll get you a drink.'

She tried to pull away. 'No, thanks, Wallis, I'm not drinking at present.'

His grip tightened and he pulled her towards the drinks table. 'All the more reason for starting now.'

He kept his arm round her waist while he bought them and held her while they drank them. He took away her empty glass and said, 'Now you're dancing with me, sweetie. No arguments. I've been waiting the whole evening for this.'

He swung her on to the floor. 'Now I've got you, I'm keeping you.'

'I'm sorry, but I'll have to return to my partner. I can't stay with you.'

'D'you mean that chap you came in with? Who is he?'

'He's my – my boy-friend.'

'So you've got a boy-friend?' He pressed his lips to her cheek. 'You never told me, darling.'

She jerked her face away. 'Don't do that. People are looking.'

'But they've been looking for months, darling. You haven't cared about that before.'

He pulled her closer and they passed Nichol with Jane. He raised his eyebrows and whispered something into Jane's ear. Jane looked at him and laughed.

'Your – er – boy-friend seems to be getting on extremely well with another woman in your absence,' Wallis commented with a grin. 'Not a faithful type, perhaps? Why should you consider his feelings, if he doesn't care about yours?' Wallis changed his tone, became matter-of-fact. 'Look, sweetie, I have to go to the staff common room to get something. The chap who joined the staff at the same time as you foolishly left a student's file there yesterday, and as I'm in tonight, I'll pop along and get it, before there's any harm done. Students' files are confidential, after all. It won't take more than a few minutes.' He pulled her behind him, but she hung back.

'You go, Wallis. I'll wait here for you.'

'You're coming with me. I'm afraid of the dark, sweetie. Those long empty corridors give me the creeps at this time of night. So come on, darling, keep me company.'

It sounded like an order, not an appeal, and she tried to twist her hand away, but he had it tight in his. As they went through the swing doors into the entrance foyer, Adrian came down the stairs and passed them on his way back to the hall. Rosalie tried to appeal to him with her eyes, but he looked away. She shivered in the cool night air. A few couples lingered in dark corners and Wallis pulled her to the stairs. He strode up them and she found it hard to keep pace with him. Her hand was still entwined with his. They reached the staff common room and he pushed her in front of him and closed the door. He fumbled at the lock and it was obvious he could not find what he was looking for. He cursed under his breath. 'No key,' she heard him mutter.

She swung round. 'Key? What do you want a key for?' She began to grow frightened. 'You came for a file, Wallis,' she reminded him.

'Did I sweetie? So I did.' He dragged a table towards the door and wedged it firmly under the door handle. 'I'll look for the file — when we've finished.'

She covered cold cheeks with hot hands. 'What do you mean? Finished what?'

'You'll soon see.' He switched off all the lights except one and advanced on her, his head slightly down.

She dodged him and ran to the door, but he was on to her before she could do a thing. 'Wallis!' Her voice rose to a shriek. 'Don't, please don't—'

But her words were cut off by his mouth. He forced her back and she struggled like a tigress. She twisted away from him, but he caught her and shook her violently. 'Stop it,' he hissed, 'or I'll really have to get rough!' She recoiled from his breath, which smelt of drink, and he imprisoned her hands. 'You've nearly driven me mad these past few weeks, you provocative little bitch. Now you're going to get what you've been asking for, and what I've been itching to give you. So you can stop playing hard to get and comply with my wishes.'

She fought him as his mouth sought hers and he slapped her face. She cried out and he slapped it again. She started sobbing. He pushed her on to a settee and she tried to use her feet to get him off. His mouth closed on hers, but she jerked her lips free. His hands went round her throat and she cried out again. There was a rattling at the door.

'Who's in there?'

Wallis covered her mouth with his hand. She lay inert for a few seconds, then somehow she moved her face and managed to sink her teeth into his flesh. He shouted with pain and she gave a strangled scream. Someone started to push at the door, once, twice, three, four times and it flew open, sending the table skidding and bouncing across the room.

Adrian stood there, rigid with anger. 'Get off that girl, Mason,' his voice was dangerously calm, then it grew louder, 'get off her and get out, you louse, or I'll kick you to the other end of this building!'

Wallis was breathing hard. He stood up, straightened his tie, then, nursing his damaged hand, walked unsteadily to the door, his head down, his clothes awry.

Adrian flung the door shut behind him. Rosalie sat up, lowered her throbbing head into her hands. Her dress was torn, her shoes had gone, her hair was a tangled mess. Adrian stood, just stood and looked at her.

She couldn't stand it. 'Why don't you say something?' she mumbled into her hands. 'Tell me what a terrible woman I am. Go on, say it!'

She heard a movement and opened her eyes to see him turn to the door. 'Adrian,' she whispered, 'don't leave me. I – I need you, Adrian. Please don't go.'

He tried the door to make sure it was securely shut, and walked slowly across to her. 'I'm not going. I wouldn't leave you now.' His voice was gentle and low. He sat beside her and put his arm round her. 'Once you came to me when I needed you. Now I'm here, when you need me. It's as simple as that.'

She hid her face again and then the shaking started. It grew so bad she turned towards him and he took her in his arms. He held her and tried to still her shivering body.

'It's n-no good, Adrian. I c-can't stop.'

'You're suffering from shock. I'll have to take action.' He retrieved her shoes and slipped them on her feet, then he pulled her gently from the settee. 'We'll go to your father's office. I've got a duplicate key.' The corridors were dim and empty and the noise from the dance barely percolated up to the first floor.

Adrian unlocked her father's door and took her in. He sat her in a chair. 'You need warmth. There's a rug in my car. I'll get it. I promise I won't be long. If you're frightened, lock the door.'

But she shook her head. She sat there, alone and shaking, just waiting. He was soon back and wrapped her tightly in the tartan rug, smiling at the result. 'You look like a granny.' She smiled back weakly. 'I'll take you home. Where are your things?'

She told him. 'You're being so g-good, Adrian.' Then she remembered. 'But you can't take me home. W-what about Jane?'

'She's well away with your gallant escort. I'll drop a word in Nichol's ear that I'm taking care of you, which will leave him free to do likewise for Jane. If you don't mind, he won't. Nor will I.'

'What will you tell my parents?'

'That you've a bad headache. Well, it's true, isn't it?' He smiled and was gone. She drooped in his absence, and tried to stop thinking, to make her mind a blank. She knew she had come to a time of decision, but knew also that she was in no fit state to make one. So she drifted into a kind of half-trance, listening to every noise, every movement which would warn her of Adrian's return.

In ten minutes, he was back. It had seemed to Rosalie like ten hours. 'It's all arranged.' He helped her with her coat, and put the rug round her again. With his arm across her shoulders, he took her out of the building which was still resounding with the beat of the music and the shrill laughter of the dancers. They passed into darkness and quiet and walked to the car park. The shaking of her body had almost stopped, but she felt exhausted. He helped her into his car and she rested her head against the side. They did not speak for the entire journey.

Adrian used his key to open the front door and took her into the lounge. He switched on the electric heater. 'You must have a drink. Brandy, I think. Your father won't mind, will he, if I help myself?'

'Of course not. You're one of the family, remember?'

He looked at her quickly, and smiled. 'You're beginning to recover, that's obvious. Now drink this. Go on, right down.'

He took away the empty glass.

'Adrian? How did you – find us? What made you look there?'

His expression darkened. 'I saw you go out with him. I kept an eye on the time. After a while I began to worry, so first I tried his room. I could see it was empty. Then I looked into the staff work room, nothing there. Finally, before I gave up, thinking you – you might have gone home with him, I tried the staff common room, arriving, luckily, at the crucial moment.'

She looked away. 'I don't know how to thank you. I'm sorry for dragging you away from the dance.' She glanced at him then. 'But you can go back now, can't you?'

'I've no intention of going back. I'll stay until your parents come home. You can go to bed. I'll do some work down here, just to pass the time.'

'But, Adrian, there's no need for you to stay ...'

'Look, Rosalie, once you looked after me. You gave up your holiday to do so. I've never forgotten it and I've never been able to repay you. Now I can, by looking after you.' He lifted her gently to her feet. 'Come on, up you go. When you're in bed, I'll bring you some hot milk.'

'You're being so good, Adrian.'

He pushed her chin upwards and looked into her eyes. Her bones seemed to melt as he said, 'Stop arguing and get up them stairs.'

She did as she was told, and when she was in bed, she called to him and he took in a cup of steaming hot milk. 'With a dash of chocolate. Is that to your taste, madam?'

As she drank it, he sat on her bed. 'Adrian?' He looked at her. 'You haven't said a word of reproach to me, although you must be thinking the most awful things about me.'

He thought for a moment, then shook his head. 'There's nothing to say, is there?' He frowned and stood up. 'You must have known it was on the cards, yet you ignored the warnings, every single one of them. The question is, and it's worrying me very much, what will you do now?'

She looked at him bleakly. 'I don't know. I just don't know. There's still Melanie.' She closed her eyes and rested her head on the pillows. He took away her empty cup.

'Shall I turn out the light?'

'Yes, please. I've got my bedside lamp. Adrian?' He smiled. 'Thank you again for all you've done.'

'That's all right. Put it down to brotherly love. After all, on your own admission, I am your adoptive brother, aren't I?'

He switched off the light, closed the door and left her.

CHAPTER EIGHT

THERE was one week of term left. The students had dispersed, there were no more lectures. Only the administrative jobs remained to be tackled and tidied up – reports to be made out, registers to get in order, timetables for the next session to be finalized.

On Monday afternoon Rosalie went to her father's room to wait for him to take her home and found Adrian there. 'Feeling better?' he asked, with a friendly smile.

'Much better, thank you.' She went into the secretary's office. 'How did you enjoy the dance, Jane? Get home all right?'

'It was wonderful, Rosalie. Nichol took me home.' She studied the typewriter keys. 'We went out together yesterday.' She looked at Rosalie uncertainly. 'Do you mind?'

'Why should I mind, Jane? It was all over between us long ago. Someone else came along for ...' She knew by the silence from the other room that Adrian was listening, 'for Nichol and you were obviously the one he had been waiting for. Give him my kind regards and I hope you'll both be very happy.'

She returned to her father's room and he was there. Adrian gave her a long look. He took his pen from his top pocket, rested a paper on her father's desk and made a few notes. 'Going away, Rosalie?' he asked, without looking up.

'Yes. For that walking holiday I missed at half-term. Only this time I'm going alone, until the last three days, then I'm joining Marion in Darlington.'

He smiled over his shoulder. 'This time I'll make quite sure I don't deprive you of it.'

Franklyn told him, 'Sarah and I will be away for the whole of August, Adrian. If the proofs of the book arrive before we go, I'll send them to you by post. Will that be all right?'

He nodded. 'Where are you going, Franklyn?'

'The south of France. Sarah has some distant relatives living there and they've invited us for a prolonged stay.' He looked at his daughter. 'Rosalie won't join us, although she was included in their invitation.'

'I told you, Dad, I want to see some of my own country this time. I've been abroad, but I haven't seen places in England like the Dales, and the Cleveland Hills.' She looked quickly at Adrian, who was now doodling on the paper he had been using for his notes. 'I'm going to Richmond and Barnard Castle and I want to see the Bowes Museum near there.'

'Youth hostelling, Rosalie?' Still Adrian would not look at her.

'Not this time. I'm doing it in comfort – staying at pubs and small hotels.'

He straightened up at last. 'Well, at least you'll have your meals cooked for you, instead of having to do it yourself.'

He pushed his pen back into his pocket, gathered up his folders and books and went home.

Friday came. It was the last day of term, and instead of going out to lunch as she had been doing all that week, to avoid Wallis, Rosalie had it with her father in the staff restaurant. Adrian was with him, as usual, and as there was an empty seat next to his, Rosalie took it. He helped her unload the tray, but after that, joined in the general conversation.

As she was drinking her coffee, he turned to her as though he had just remembered she was there. 'Enjoy your lunch?'

'Yes, thank you.'

His attention lingered and she asked him, 'How's your radio going? Is it still functioning properly?'

'Very well, thanks. I've boxed the two speakers now, and stained and varnished the wood. They look very smart.' He paused and said, 'You wouldn't be hinting that you'd like to hear it again?'

She laughed. 'That wasn't what I intended, but if you

asked me, I wouldn't refuse.'

'M'm. I'll have to think about it.' He picked up his empty cup and looked into it as if trying to read non-existent tea leaves. 'Mrs. Fields keeps asking how my young lady is, and says she doesn't come to see me very often.'

'What do you tell her?'

'That she's well, and that I go to her house and also see her at work. Well,' he challenged, 'it's true, isn't it?'

She coloured and her pulses raced. 'Is it?' She steadied her voice and said, 'But wouldn't it have been a good opportunity to tell her the truth – that you haven't got a girl-friend, or that we've quarrelled?'

'It might. But she seems to be taking such a motherly interest in us both, I haven't the heart to disillusion her.'

'I think you'll have to be cruel to be kind,' she joked. 'The longer you put off telling her, the worse it will be when you do.'

He toyed with his teaspoon. 'If you come to my flat and hear my radio again, it will only reinforce her in her conviction that we're sweethearts.' He looked into her eyes. 'Won't it?'

She looked away, dazzled. 'Yes. So I'd better not come, had I?'

'No.' She was blinded by the sudden darkness.

Wallis came in, his eyes searching the tables. He spotted Rosalie, then joined the queue at the lunch-counter.

She excused herself from her companions and left the restaurant.

That afternoon, Rosalie called in to make some last minute arrangements with Marion. They were intending to meet in Darlington in about ten days' time and catch a train to Durham. They exchanged holiday addresses, so that they could contact each other in an emergency, and as they talked, Rosalie looked apprehensively at Wallis's door. Marion noticed and asked, 'Do you want to see Mr. Mason? He's somewhere in the building.'

Rosalie shook her head hurriedly. She had managed to avoid him all the week, and whenever she had seen him walking along the corridor, she had usually slipped into an empty classroom until he had passed. She began to worry about Melanie, but could not bring herself to talk to him.

As she left Marion's office, Adrian was walking past. 'Ah, Rosalie, I'm glad I've seen you. I wanted to say good-bye. I'm off to my mother's on Sunday morning.'

She tried to smile. 'For the entire holiday, Adrian?'

'Yes, six weeks.'

'It's – it's a long time, isn't it?'

He stared out of the window overlooking the college playing fields and frowned. 'Yes.'

'I shall only be away a couple of weeks.'

'What will you do for the rest of the time?'

'Oh, moon around at home, probably. Or I might even take myself to the Lakes for a few days.'

'I see.' There was a long silence, and she could feel the beginnings of tears somewhere inside her. He seemed to draw himself upright with an effort. 'Well, good-bye.'

She held out her hand and he took it between his. 'I'll see you again next term, Adrian,' she said.

'Rosalie,' the pressure of his hands increased, 'will you – will you . . .'

'Excuse me,' a voice said beside them, 'but may I get into my office? You're blocking the doorway.'

Wallis Mason surveyed them coldly. Adrian dropped her hand and they moved. 'Miss Parham, would you kindly come in for a few minutes? I wish to speak to you.' Wallis went into his room.

'Rosalie.' Adrian gripped her shoulder. She looked at him sadly, ignoring the warning note in his voice.

'Good-bye, Adrian,' she said, and went into Wallis's room, closing the door on the rigid figure outside.

'Rosalie, sit down.' Wallis barely raised his eyes. 'I'd like to talk to you.'

'I'll stand, thank you.'

He shrugged. 'As you wish.' He hesitated, as if unsure

of what he wanted to say. 'I suppose it's no use saying I'm sorry for what happened at the dance, or expecting you to understand if I tell you I was the worse for drink, having imbibed practically the whole evening?'

He darted a look at her and dropped his eyes. She could find nothing to say. 'I'd like to explain,' he went on, 'if you'll be good enough to listen, something that the rumour-mongers couldn't possibly know.' He indicated a chair. 'Please, Rosalie, sit down and bear with me for just a few minutes longer.'

His tone was so subdued and he was so different from his usual brash self that she complied. 'Thank you,' he murmured, and after a moment or two, continued, 'What is not generally known, for obvious reasons, is that the woman I married was a cold-blooded creature. I lied when I told you she had gone off with another man. She wanted no man, not even her husband.

'After Melanie was born, my wife – turned frigid. I'm a normal man. The two just don't go together. We didn't.' He chose his words carefully, and he kept his eyes down. Rosalie could see it was costing him an effort to speak so frankly. 'Those people who criticize men like me are usually happily married and, in their smug content with their lot, turn virtuous and stand in judgment on others less fortunate then themselves.'

He raised tired eyes. 'No one who has not experienced it can know what it's like to be married to a woman who, without mercy or pity, repulses your every approach. It makes a mockery of married life, of love itself.' He paused and ran a hand across his eyes. 'You came along. I was attracted to you, and although I knew you were different from others I've known, I didn't give up hope.'

He looked at her appealingly now. 'For Melanie's sake, Rosalie, I beg you to come home with me this evening and see her. She's fretting for you. I've hardly had a minute's peace since last week-end from her demands to see you. Will you come – please?'

She had to sort things out in her mind. She really needed time, but knew she could not have it. If she went with him, what had she to lose? Nothing more, surely?

She had already lost the only thing she could ever want – the love of the man she loved, not that she had ever had that love in the first place.

She forced out at last, 'Thank you for telling me this, Wallis. I'll try to understand, but you must realize that everything I did was for Melanie's sake. I subordinated my pride and my self-respect, I forfeited my reputation and – and certainly my future happiness,' her voice faltered, 'for her. It was for no other reason.' She stopped and came to a decision. 'Yes, I'll go with you, just to see her.'

'And will you trust me?'

She paused and whispered, 'I'll try.'

So, later that day, after the evening meal, Wallis called for her and took her to his home again. Melanie gave her a rapturous welcome. They played together as before, and Rosalie bathed her and put her to bed. Her eyes were shining because her 'second mummy' had come back.

'Perhaps,' she whispered in Rosalie's ear as she bent to kiss her good night, 'my real mummy will come back again, too.'

Next day, Saturday, Rosalie went there to tea. She stayed again until Melanie was in bed, and later, Wallis took her home. He held on to her hand just before she left him.

'I want to tell you, Rosalie, that I've instructed my solicitor to try to trace my wife, with a – with a view to a possible reconciliation.' He put her hand from him. 'In all the circumstances, I have little alternative but to try.'

Now she covered his hand with hers. 'Wallis, that's wonderful news. May I say I hope that this time, if you come together again, things will work out better for you?'

He shrugged indifferently. 'Who knows what the future holds?' He raised her hand to his lips. 'Have a good holiday.' He smiled for the first time that day and drove away.

Her mother met her in the hall. 'Adrian called,' she said. 'He asked me if you were in.' Rosalie could not hide the disappointment which swept over her. 'When I told

146

him you were not, he asked me if you had gone to Wallis Mason's house. I tried to pretend I didn't know, but he made me tell him the truth, darling. He was very angry when he heard you had. But I couldn't lie to him, could I?'

Rosalie shrugged hopelessly and shook her head.

Sarah went on, 'He said he hadn't come to see you, anyway. Then he went home. We won't be seeing him now for six weeks.'

'I had to go with Wallis, Mum. Melanie had been fretting for me, although I don't suppose anyone will believe me.'

'I do, darling. Does that help?'

'It helps a lot, Mum.' Rosalie kissed her cheek and went wearily upstairs.

Monday morning dawned bright with a promise of sunshine. Rosalie was having breakfast when the postman delivered the proofs of her father's book. He went into the kitchen while she was washing up the breakfast dishes and stood beside her.

He cleared his throat. 'My dear, since your journey will be taking you in the vicinity of Adrian's mother's house, where he's staying, it occurred to me that it might be better if you could take these proofs to him personally, rather than risk sending them through the post.' He cleared his throat again. 'It would be so much safer, wouldn't it, and you would see – I mean, I would feel happier if I knew they were in safe keeping.'

Rosalie suppressed a smile, and turned to her father with a bland expression. 'Provided they'll go in my haversack, Dad, and won't get damaged, I suppose I could take them.'

'Of course, dear, if it would be taking you out of your way ...'

'Well, it would a bit, but I don't mind.' Then she frowned. 'I'm not sure if Adrian would be pleased to see me, but I suppose I'd have to risk that. I need only stay a short time, after all.'

Her father seemed pleased. 'Well, I'll leave them on the

dining-room table for you to pack. Now don't forget them, will you?'

She smiled at her parents' little ruse and a sweet thrill of anticipation raced through her. She kissed them good-bye, wishing them a safe journey to the south of France, and told them not to worry about her. 'I'm a big girl now,' she laughed. 'I can look after myself.'

All the same, as she walked along the road and turned to give them a final wave, she felt just a little lost and had to still a vague but disturbing presentiment about her im-mediate future, which pecked, bird-like, at the back of her mind.

Interwoven into the fabric of her enjoyment of the hol-iday she spent in the Yorkshire Dales was a thread of excitement which gave the incomparable scenery around her an even greater beauty because, in just a few more days, she would be seeing Adrian again.

She wandered through Wensleydale and visited the falls of Aysgarth, and looked with wonder at Hardraw, that waterfall with a rounded backcloth of rock, and watched people walking underneath the narrow column of water as it spurted over and dropped from a height of nearly a hundred feet.

She moved north to Swaledale and admired its beauties and arrived at last at Barnard Castle, knowing all the time that she was getting nearer to Adrian. She stayed two nights at a small hotel in the main street, explored the castle remains, walked by the river and visited the Bowes Museum set in impressive ornamental gardens about half a mile from the town.

When she settled her bill at the hotel, she borrowed a timetable from the proprietor and decided to catch the early afternoon bus to Middleton-in-Teesdale, about ten miles away. She had a sandwich lunch by the river, fini-shing in good time to get the bus. The journey was pleasant and relaxing. The hills, rolling into the distance, were punctuated by sweeping valleys and the rock-en-crusted river below, and the beauty of the landscape helped to soothe away the apprehension which had begun to build up inside her as to the kind of welcome Adrian might give her. All the same, she felt a growing excitement at the thought of meeting his mother at last.

The bus drew up near the car park. She got out, stretched her cramped limbs and stood on the pavement, with her rucksack at her feet, and glanced uncertainly up and down the main street. The scrap of paper with Adrian's address on it was in her pocket, but she knew the number of the house and the name of the road by heart.

She asked the way and was directed left along the road and left again, and she would be there. Her heartbeats quickened as she followed the directions and then the house was there in front of her. It seemed very small, being part of a long terrace of similar dwellings, all built of grey stone. There was a tiny garden, and a wrought-iron gate added an amusing touch of luxury. The bright blue front door smelled of new paint and as she lifted the heavy knocker, the bang resounded up and down the street.

She looked round nervously, certain that all the neighbours must be staring out, but there was not a disturbed net curtain or an inquisitive face in sight. A few minutes passed and she began to think the house was empty. Then she heard a movement in the hall and the door opened.

A grey-haired woman stood there, her comfortable plumpness echoed in the roundness of her face and the warmth in her eyes. Rosalie recognized her immediately. This was the snapshot on Adrian's table come to life. She gave an inquiring half-smile. Rosalie hesitated, feeling extraordinarily shy.

Then she said, 'Mrs. Crayford? My name is Rosalie Parham. Is Adrian in?'

The door was drawn open wide and the smile broadened into one of unmistakable welcome. 'Come in, come in, my dear. How nice of you to call. I'm so glad to meet you at last. I'll get my son. He's upstairs.'

But her son was already on the landing. He was looking down as though he could not believe his eyes. There was a fixed and puzzled stare on his face as he came down to the hall. Mrs. Crayford helped Rosalie remove her rucksack. 'Put it in the corner, my dear, and come in. You must surely want a cup of tea.'

She looked at her son, apparently wondering at his silence. She saw his frown and told him, just a little impatiently, 'Put the kettle on, son. Miss Parham must be tired with the bus journey. That is how you came, dear, isn't it?'

Rosalie nodded. 'I caught the bus at Barnard Castle.'

She looked at Adrian and could not understand why he had still not greeted her. His mother noticed his lack of manners. 'My son looks as if he's seen a ghost. For some reason, he's struck dumb.'

Adrian took the hint and seemed to jerk himself out of a trance. 'Hallo, Rosalie. Why have you come?'

She wanted to cry at the lack of welcome in his voice. 'I've brought the proofs of two chapters of the book, the ones my father told you he would send by post. He changed his mind at the last minute and thought it would be safer if I brought them here myself.'

'I see.' He was off-hand. 'I'll put the kettle on.'

She struggled with a desire to burst into tears. She had not expected to be welcomed with open arms, but she certainly had not foreseen this. His mother called her into the lounge. 'Make yourself comfortable, Rosalie. You don't mind if I call you that? It's how my son always refers to you.' She patted the cushion next to her and Rosalie sat down, a little on edge, despite her pleasantness. 'You mustn't let my son's attitude upset you, my dear. He's like most unmarried men of his age – his corners need filing down!'

'I'm not upset, Mrs. Crayford. It's just . . .' Desperately she looked around the room, taking in the thick pile of the fitted carpet, the good quality furniture and the heavily-lined curtains. 'It's very pleasant in here. Do you get a lot of sun, or—'

'This room faces west, so we get it in the afternoon.' She looked outside. 'What a lovely day it is. Have you been lucky with the weather? Tell me about it.'

So Rosalie told her that of the ten days she had so far

spent on her travels, only two had been wet, and even then she had been able to get out for short walks. Adrian brought in the tray.

'Just like old times,' he flashed at her, with his first smile since she had arrived. 'Cups, saucers and a tray. Feel at home?'

She smiled back. 'Well, it's nice to be waited on.'

Mrs. Crayford gave her a questioning look and Adrian enlightened her. She listened with growing surprise to his account of Rosalie's role in her parents' household. 'And you have a full-time job, too? With all the usual work and preparation to do at home? It's a wonder you're not worn out. Then you go on a walking holiday, instead of resting!'

'If she's here more than half an hour, Mother, you won't be able to keep her out of your kitchen. She seems to gravitate naturally in that direction. Second nature to her.'

'Of course she'll stay more than half an hour. I've been waiting months to meet you. You're not getting away from me as quickly as that! What are your plans, my dear?'

Rosalie answered vaguely. 'Oh, I – I thought I'd stay in a pub in Middleton for the night, and look round some of the beauty spots tomorrow morning. In the evening, I'm going to Darlington to meet Marion,' she explained. 'I'm spending the last few days of my holiday with her. She's visiting relatives there, and—' She took the cup of tea which Adrian had poured out, and accepted a biscuit from his mother.

'So you're more or less free to do what you like until then?'

Rosalie nodded. Mrs. Crayford looked at Adrian. 'Well, go on, son, invite her to stay the night.'

'Me? It's your house, Mother.' He had a sudden thought. 'Anyway, where would she sleep? We've only got two bedrooms.'

'In your bed, of course.'

He nearly exploded. 'In *my* bed?'

'You know what I mean, son. You can sleep down here

in your sleeping bag, and Rosalie can have your bed.'

He walked restlessly round the room, tutting. 'Well, I like that! Giving away my bed . . .' But there was a softer note in his voice.

'Mrs. Crayford, please don't let Adrian put himself out for me. I'm quite prepared to stay at a pub, and move on in the morning. I don't want to be a nuisance.'

'Don't be stupid, Rosalie,' Adrian cut in, 'of course you can stay. I've given up my bed before to others.'

'There's no need to snap her head off, son. As you said, it's my house and she's my guest.' She studied Rosalie's face as she took the empty cup. 'You know, Adrian, your description of Rosalie was so wrong. Where's all this sophistication you keep talking about?'

He looked at Rosalie then, seeing her wind-worried hair, her flushed cheeks, and blue slacks and brown windcheater which was unzipped and showing a white tee-shirt underneath. She dropped her eyes under his scrutiny and he turned away. 'There are so many Rosalies, I've lost count. The variety is so great, I never know which one I'm going to find next.'

His mother gave him a penetrating look and covered Rosalie's hand with hers. 'So it's all settled and you're staying?'

'Well, it's very kind of you, Mrs. Crayford. If you're quite sure . . .'

'She's staying, Mother.' Adrian gathered the crockery and put it back on the tray. 'Here's the kitchen, Rosalie,' he called over his shoulder. 'Would you like to borrow one of my mother's aprons?'

'She'll do no such thing, my boy. She's on holiday. She won't set foot in there.'

'You won't be able to keep her out. See,' he turned as Rosalie hovered in the doorway, 'she's in here already.' He tossed her a tea towel. 'You dry. For once our roles are reversed.'

His mother was indignant, and took the towel from Rosalie's hands. 'You just leave them on the draining-board. She's coming upstairs with me to see the room she'll be sleeping in.'

'Then she'll get a shock. You can't see my bed for radio parts. I'm taking one of my early efforts to bits and it's spread all over the place. Mind where you walk,' he called upstairs after them. 'The floor's littered with parts of the radio.'

'He's right, you know. I'm so sorry, my dear. I had no idea it was in this mess.'

'We weren't expecting company, remember,' Adrian said, drying his hands and coming up the stairs two at a time. 'Don't touch a thing. I'll do all the clearing that's necessary.' He looked askance at Rosalie and smiled. 'Just enough to let her get into bed.'

'Suits me,' she answered, 'just as long as I don't find any in the bed.'

Adrian looked thoughtful. 'Now that's an idea . . .'

His mother snorted. 'Don't listen to him. I'll go and find some clean sheets.'

'Clean sheets? She can use mine.'

She tutted impatiently. 'Men!' she said, and went out.

There was a silence which grew so painful Rosalie felt she had to break it. 'Thank you for giving up your bed, Adrian. It certainly wasn't my intention to put you or your mother out like this.'

He was frowning and concentrating on something in his hand. 'It doesn't matter.'

'I'll go, if you want me to. It's still not too late for me to find somewhere else for the night.'

'You can't go. My mother would want to know why.'

There was silence again, and she stood, hands in her trouser pockets, watching him. His mother returned.

'Have you cleared that bed yet, son?'

He picked up the last few items and his mother stripped the bed down to the mattress. Rosalie helped. 'There's no need to go to all this bother, Mrs. Crayford.'

'It's no bother, dear. I'm only too glad to have you here. Aren't we, Adrian?'

'If you say so, Mother, yes.' He was busy with his radio.

'Take no notice of my son's bad manners,' Mrs Crayford commented.

'I'm never bad-mannered. I merely say what I think.'

'Well, in certain circumstances that could be construed as bad manners.' She bustled out to get pillowcases.

Rosalie said quietly, and her voice trembled despite her efforts to control it, 'Don't worry, Adrian, I'll leave first thing in the morning. I never outstay my welcome, however short that welcome may be.'

Still he did not speak, just went on fiddling with his radio.

During the evening, Mrs. Crayford made up for her son's lack of good spirits. She encouraged Rosalie to talk, listened with interest to everything she said, tried to draw Adrian into the conversation and she was so determined, she eventually succeeded.

Rosalie found herself relaxing for the first time since her arrival. The meal was over, the washing-up finished. Rosalie had insisted on helping with that, despite Mrs. Crayford's protests and Adrian's sardonic laughter at his mother's attempts to keep her out of the kitchen.

She had been shown the garden and admired its order and colour. She had seen the rest of the house which, small and old though it was, had been furnished and decorated so tastefully that its size and age seemed irrelevant.

Now they were talking. 'Tell me about your family, Rosalie. I know your father's at the college, of course, and he's Adrian's department head. They seem to get on well together, don't they? And what about your mother?'

Rosalie glanced at Adrian who seemed to be absorbed in a technical magazine dealing with radio and television. 'My mother is a university lecturer,' she said. 'She's very clever. She – she would have been a Ph.D. if I hadn't come along.'

'Oh, I'm sure she would rather have had a daughter than another degree.'

'Well, I—' Rosalie looked at Adrian's disinterested

profile. 'Yes, I expect so,' she added lamely.

'I'd have given a great deal to have had a daughter as well as a son.' She smiled. 'But it wasn't to be.' She glanced at Adrian. 'I shall have to rely on my son to provide me with one, one day, won't I, Adrian?'

'What?' He looked up with a frown. 'Oh yes, Mother, one day. When I'm growing old and grey and get fed up with being a bachelor.'

'What a pity, son, then I won't be here to enjoy my daughter-in-law, will I?'

'Of course you will. You'll live for ever.'

She laughed. 'He's a good son, Rosalie.' She paused. 'But he'd make an even better father.' Her eyes grew a little sad as she dwelt on his serious face. Then she sighed and asked Rosalie in a lighter tone, 'Where are you making for tomorrow?'

Rosalie's answer was vague. She did not want tomorrow to come because she would have to leave Adrian behind. 'Oh, I thought of looking for that waterfall not far from here – I think it's called High Force. Marion told me it's a sight not be be missed.'

Adrian looked up at last. 'How do you intend to get there?'

'I've really no idea. I thought there might be a bus.'

'It's better to go by car.'

'It probably is, but apart from public transport, all I've got is my legs.'

Adrian's eyes contemplated the objects under discussion, cleared his throat and resumed his reading.

His mother turned to him. 'You're free tomorrow, Adrian. You can take Rosalie to High Force. In fact,' she went on before he could answer, 'you could spend the day with her and take her to other beauty spots. I could give you a packed lunch and you could have tea at the High Force Hotel. How about it, son?'

His doubtful eyes looked at Rosalie and she desperately tried to hide her mounting excitement. 'Well?' His tone was belligerent and she shrank from it.

'No, it really doesn't matter.' She hoped she had been able to disguise the disappointment which swamped her.

'If there's no bus to the place, I'll go somewhere else. Or travel straight to Darlington and have a look at the shops.'

Mrs. Crayford eased herself off the couch and went to the bookshelves. She drew out a book and opened it. 'This is a guide to the Yorkshire dales and fells.' She thrust it under her son's nose. 'Show this to Rosalie. Show her a photo of High Force, then she'll know she mustn't miss it while she's so near. Take my place on the couch next to her. Come on, son.'

He must have sensed that his casual attitude was beginning to irritate her. He sighed long-sufferingly, stretched, put aside his magazine and walked lazily across to fling himself down beside Rosalie. He opened the guide book and motioned to her to move closer to him. Their heads almost touched as she leaned across to look at the pages which flicked through his fingers, and she struggled to hide the tingling excitement his nearness aroused in her.

He pointed to a photograph which occupied a whole page. 'There's High Force.' He read aloud from the book, 'The river Tees races fifteen miles from Crossfell, which is nearly three thousand feet in height, and the rushing water drops seventy feet into a deep, stone-walled chasm. The fall is divided by a rock sixty-three feet high, the upper of which is basalt with vertical joints, while the lower limestone is in strongly marked horizontal layers.' He smiled. 'Have all those technicalities put you off, or do you still want to see it?'

'More than ever.' She gazed at the picture of the waterfall. 'It looks marvellous.' She looked at him and their faces were within touching distance. He stared into her eyes, then drew away.

'You must take her, Adrian.' His mother was watching them. 'She may not be in this area again for years.'

He shifted towards Rosalie and put his arm round her shoulders. 'In that case, I'd better take her tomorrow.' He pulled her even closer so that she could see the guide book more clearly. One look at Rosalie's face must have told Mrs. Crayford all she wanted to know about her feelings

156

for her son. With his right hand, he turned the pages, stopping now and then to let her look at the photographs. She stretched her hand across him to hold the pages down, and when he came to the end of the book, he snapped it shut.

'There are so many lovely places,' Rosalie commented, 'I shall leave the area having seen only a fraction of them.'

'Then you'll just have to come another year, dear.' Mrs. Crayford stood at the door. 'It's getting late. I'll make a hot drink. What would you like, Rosalie, milk, chocolate or what?'

Adrian tightened his fingers round her arm. 'She likes hot milk with a dash of chocolate, don't you? Preferably sitting up in bed looking pretty.'

'Does she indeed?' His mother looked suitably shocked. 'And how do you know that, my son?'

He smiled at her wickedly. 'Now that would be telling, Mother.' He lifted his hand and ruffled Rosalie's hair. 'I was conducting what might be called a rescue operation, and being very brotherly. So you needn't look so horrified.'

'Oh, I see. Well, hot chocolate it shall be.' She went into the kitchen.

'Can I help you, Mrs. Crayford?' Rosalie called after her.

'No, no, thank you, my dear. You stay comfortable, where you are.'

As soon as she had gone, Adrian took his arm away and got up. He pushed the book back into place on the shelf, then he sat in the armchair and resumed his reading.

Rosalie walked aimlessly to the window. It was dark now. The long northern twilight had ended. She could just make out the outline of the houses opposite, and there were lights in the windows. The street was narrow, but there was a friendly feeling about the place which seemed to be missing in the south. When she turned back to the room, the friendly feeling had gone. There was a distinct chill in the atmosphere, and she shivered.

'Cold?' Adrian asked. So he wasn't entirely oblivious of

her presence. 'I'll switch on the electric fire. It gets chilly in these northern parts even in late July.'

They drank their milk and chatted and Mrs. Crayford saw Rosalie up to bed. She gave her a towel and told her to ask for anything she might want, like a nightdress, but Rosalie assured her she had a couple with her. They said good night, and Mrs. Crayford wished her pleasant dreams. When she had gone, Rosalie realized that Adrian had not even said good night.

As she lay in the darkness, she looked round his room, trying to work out what the different shapes were. His presence was everywhere and she turned on to her side with a sigh and went to sleep at last.

CHAPTER NINE

It seemed only a few minutes after closing her eyes that she heard a tap on the door. But it was next morning and she had slept soundly through the night.

'Rosalie, may I come in?' Without waiting for an answer, Adrian opened the door. He was in his dressing gown and walked across the room holding two cups of tea. Rosalie sat up quickly and took a cup from him. His eyes swept over her. 'Even first thing in the morning you manage to look pretty. Don't know how you do it.'

'You seem to hold it against me. You say it as though it annoys you.'

'Do I? Sorry.' He walked to the window, opened the curtains and drank his tea, staring into the garden. 'It's a lovely day. You're lucky with the weather. You'll be seeing High Force at its best.'

She said with a grin, 'Won't your mother worry about you being in here with me?'

He half-turned. 'You mean propriety and so on? Good heavens, no. She wants me to get married, haven't you guessed?' He gave a short, cynical laugh. 'She probably thinks this is a preliminary to my proposing to you.' He put down his empty cup. 'I suppose I shall have to marry one day, if only to satisfy her craving for grandchildren.'

His cynicism hurt so much she wanted to hurt him back. She didn't care what she said, as long as it inflicted a wound as deep as the one he had just inflicted on her.

'Yes,' she said, putting down her cup and looking at him speculatively, 'you should get married. You should find yourself a nice little yes-woman, who would pander to your self-esteem and your every whim. Someone you could use as a doormat, who wouldn't mind your lack of manners, your coldness and your calculating scientific mind.'

He moved slowly to the bedside, his eyes tearing her

apart. 'Carry on enumerating the finer points of my character. It's really doing my ego a power of good.'

'But surely your ego is fed to bursting point by the superiority of your intellect and by your academic achievements. You hardly need me to tell you how incredibly attractive and clever you are...'

She tried to duck under the bedclothes, but he threw himself on the bed and caught her wrists and although she struggled, he forced her arms back against the pillows. His blazing eyes examined her in excruciating detail as she lay there helpless.

'You know what you're asking for, don't you?' he bit out. His face came down and his lips covered hers. His arms slipped round her and she could feel the hardness of his fingers biting into her flesh. His kiss was long, savage and uncompromising. It demanded and got complete surrender. He lifted his head slowly, breathing hard. 'And I've a damned good mind to give it to you.'

She was afraid now, afraid of the clamouring emotions he had aroused in her, afraid of his cold passion and afraid, above all, because he could look at her like that and yet not love her. She closed her eyes to shut his out, and rubbed her wrists where he had gripped them. 'On second thoughts,' he drawled, standing up, 'it's hardly the right circumstances. It'll be all the better for keeping.'

She opened her eyes which were damp with tears. 'Why do you hate me, Adrian?'

He smiled as he looked down at her. 'So I hate you? Oh dear, do my feelings show so much? But surely the sentiment is mutual, Rosalie? Isn't it?'

She closed her eyes again. If he looked into them now, she knew he would see the answer to his question.

'Adrian,' his mother called from downstairs, 'it's taking you a long time to kiss Rosalie good morning. You'd better come out and let her get dressed. You're not married to her yet, you know.'

He raised his eyebrows and smiled. 'See what I mean?' He strolled to the door. 'You'd better get up. It's my bed you're in, remember. I might decide to reclaim it from you by occupying it without prior notice and before you've had a chance to vacate it.'

He walked out and closed the door on her mutinous eyes.

After breakfast, Rosalie went upstairs to collect her belongings. Adrian was in the bedroom and she apologized for intruding. She rolled up her nightdress and pushed it into her rucksack. She peeled off the bedclothes and folded the sheets, found Adrian's and remade the bed to save his mother the trouble. As she drew the quilt over the eiderdown, Adrian mumbled his thanks. She stood for a moment watching him. He turned and saw her.

'Go on, ask me – what am I doing?'

'All right, what are you doing?'

'Rebuilding a transistor radio I made some time ago. I'm improving on the original design.'

She looked duly impressed.

'Have you got one?' he asked.

'A transistor radio? Yes, but it's so old it's falling to bits and I've stuck it together with adhesive tape.'

He winced. 'Sacrilege!' After a moment, he said, 'When I've finished this, would you like to have it?'

'I – I'd love to have it, Adrian. But – but would it work, and how much . . .'

'Any more insults? Of course it will work. Everything I make works. And I'd give it to you as a gift. With my love.' He flashed her a mocking smile which she tried to ignore and thanked him.

'When will it be finished?'

'Oh, in a few days. I could either send it to you by post, or keep it until I see you at the college next term.'

She moved away from him. 'I leave it to you.'

She lifted her rucksack and hitched it over her shoulder. 'Will you be long? Your mother's made the sandwiches and a flask of tea, and they're ready for you to pack.'

'What's the time – nearly eleven o'clock? We could have coffee, then leave.'

She nodded and went downstairs. She offered to make the coffee, but Mrs. Crayford would not let her, so she sat in the kitchen and they chatted about Rosalie's parents, about her work at the college and about the subjects she had read for her degree.

As Rosalie watched Adrian's mother move about the kitchen, saw the sympathy which had etched lines of compassion in her pleasant face, so like her son's, and felt the aura of warmth which her motherliness radiated around her, she knew it was just as she had imagined it would be when eventually she met this mother of Adrian's. She revelled in the give-and-take of views, the feeling that they had a common bond of ideas and interests. That photograph in its silver frame on Adrian's table had come to life, and the promise it had held so many weeks ago had been fulfilled.

'Call Adrian, dear, will you? When you've had your coffee, you must be off.'

Adrian joined them in the front room, wearing a thick tweedy jacket over his open-necked shirt.

'Where will you take Rosalie first?' his mother asked.

'We'll make for Winch Bridge, have lunch there and go to High Force afterwards.'

'You'll have tea at the hotel, won't you? Make sure she has a good meal inside her before you take her on to Darlington, son.'

'Are you taking me to Darlington, Adrian? Please don't bother, I could go by bus. It's such a long way for you to drive.'

'It's no trouble to him, Rosalie. I insist he takes you.'

'It's not as far as you think,' he said. 'I'd know the way there blindfold, I've done it so often.'

'Do you intend going anywhere farther afield?' his mother wanted to know.

'There won't be time. Can't achieve too much in a day.'

'Rosalie will just have to come again, won't she, Adrian?'

'Perhaps.'

His mother frowned and shook her head hopelessly at Rosalie. He tossed the last few drops of coffee down his throat and stood up. 'Time we were off. Where are those sandwiches?' He went into the kitchen.

'You've been so kind, Mrs. Crayford. Saying "thank you" doesn't seem adequate.'

'It's really I who should thank you for the joy of your company, my dear.' She smiled sadly. 'There's a great emptiness somewhere inside me that's crying out to be filled by a girl such as you.'

Impulsively, Rosalie put her arms round her.

'My son's so obstinate,' she went on. 'He's so slow about things that matter, so – so stupid at times. The best in life will pass him by and some day, when he's too old, he'll realize what he's missed.'

Adrian came out of the kitchen and stood in the doorway, watching as his mother drew Rosalie's face down and kissed her cheeks. There were tears in her eyes when Rosalie kissed her back.

'It's been wonderful meeting you, Mrs. Crayford. It's meant so much to me!'

She pressed Rosalie's hand. 'Have a good day, both of you.' She waved as they got into the car and drove away.

For some time after they had left the house, there was a heavy silence. Rosalie felt she had to make contact with him somehow. 'Your mother was everything I imagined she would be, Adrian.'

He answered coolly, 'She appeared to return the compliment.'

'You can put me down anywhere you like, Adrian.' She almost choked over the words. 'You don't have to waste your entire day with me. It wasn't my idea.'

He gave an exaggerated sigh, checked in the driving mirror and pulled up at the side of the road. He turned off the ignition and swivelled round. 'Let's get this straight before we go any farther. If you want,' he spoke tersely, 'we can go our separate ways.'

Her eyes burnt with dryness as she stared back at him. 'Is that what *you* want?'

'I'm asking you. If you dislike me so much you can't stand my undiluted company for a few hours, then all right, we'll part now. Otherwise, I'll play along with you.

I'm game either way, but you make the choice. Do we separate now – or go together?'

'We – we go together.'

'Right. That's all I wanted to know.' He started the engine, released the handbrake and drove on.

She forced her thoughts outwards, seeking balm from the beauty of the landscape. The countryside opened out into green fields and distant hills. The road climbed and now and then she caught a tantalizing glimpse of the sparkling, winding river Tees below.

'This is wonderful,' she breathed, her spirits rising in spite of herself. 'I had no idea there was so much beauty in this part of England.'

'Then you've a lot to learn, haven't you?' he taunted. 'I agree, this is good, but there's much that is better. You must have seen quite a lot on your travels this holiday which equals if not surpasses this in beauty. If you want to see real grandeur, you should go on to the wild moorland.'

'I've seen a bit of it, but don't forget I was on foot, and there's a limit to the distance you can cover in a day. In a car, you can penetrate so much deeper.'

'Then you'll just have to take my mother up on her invitation and come again some time, won't you? But I don't guarantee I'll be here to take you out.'

She bit hard on her lip, pressing down on the wound inside her to stop the anguish spurting from it.

They drove into a small village called Newbiggin and Adrian parked the car off the road. 'This is our first stop. We've got a bit of walking to do.' He reached to the back for their rucksacks, and they got out. He locked the car. 'This way,' he said, and walked on in front.

They went across a field, climbed over a narrow stile which broke into a drystone wall, and walked in single file along a path which descended towards the river. They half ran down a grassy bank, and there it was, a miniature suspension bridge across the Tees. A short distance along the river to the right was a series of small, rushing waterfalls, the white, hissing foam tinged with brown.

Rosalie read a notice painted on a board. Only one

person at a time, it said, should walk across the bridge. It seemed so flimsy and as she looked at it, it moved gently in the breeze. She glanced apprehensively at Adrian. 'Is it really safe?'

He laughed. 'Of course. This isn't the original bridge. That was built in 1704 by the lead miners who needed to cross here, and they did claim it was the earliest suspension bridge in Europe. It was damaged in the great floods later that century, but repaired. Just to cheer you up, early in the nineteenth century a main chain snapped while people were crossing it. A young man was drowned. But that was a very long time ago. Now, are you going first?' He grinned at her nervousness.

'No, you go first, please.'

'All right, but once I'm across, you're on your own.'

He walked down to the bridge and started cautiously across it. He stopped and called teasingly over his shoulder, 'Testing, testing, just testing.' It swayed with his weight and her hand flew to her mouth.

'Now you,' he called from the other bank.

She hesitated, put an exploratory foot on to the bridge, both feet, then started walking. The river rushed by underneath and the bridge moved as she moved. She gripped the flexible handrail and kept her eyes on the laughing figure at the other end.

When she set foot on firm land once more, he said, 'Quite an adventure for a scared little girl, wasn't it?'

'I certainly wouldn't like to cross it in a high gale,' she commented.

'I'd agree with you there. But when I was a young boy, I used to come here with my mother for picnics and I went on that bridge and tugged at it until it swayed alarmingly. I did it to frighten her and I certainly succeeded!'

'It sounds as though you were naughty when you were young.'

'I was. I'm a good boy now, though.' His eyes crept over her. 'Too good, sometimes.' He glanced around. 'Here's a clearing where we can sit for lunch.'

The rucksack slipped off his shoulders and he removed

his jacket and spread it out for them to sit on. As it was so warm, Rosalie took off her windcheater and threw it down. Adrian stretched his legs on the grass and rested on his elbow, while she ran down the slope towards the river with her camera. She gazed at the waterfalls, listened to them rushing and tumbling over the boulders. She held her camera to her eye and took two or three photographs from different angles, then she wandered back, to find that Adrian had been watching her. Without warning, she snapped him.

'You,' he said lazily, narrowing his eyes, 'deserve a spank for that. I'll do the same to you some time, when you're least expecting it.'

She bent down and carefully tucked her camera away in her rucksack. She straightened up and walked across to get the food from Adrian's bag. Her foot caught in the rucksack straps and she tripped and fell towards him. He caught her as she landed face down across his legs.

'By heaven,' he muttered, 'this is surely too good an opportunity to miss. Shall I spank her? I'm very tempted.'

She struggled, but he forced her to be still. 'On second thoughts, perhaps not.' He gave her a single sharp slap which stung as he turned her over.

'I'm terribly sorry I fell on you,' she said, going pink, and trying to raise herself.

'My pleasure entirely.'

She tried again to get up, but he held her down, so she lay still and gazed up at him.

'Do you know,' he said softly, 'every time you look at me, your eyes ask me to kiss you.'

'It's not true, Adrian.'

'Oh, but it is, my sweet. You can't see the expression in them. Well, I'm always willing to oblige a lady with my lips, if not my heart.' He swung her round until she was beneath him and he kissed her until she cried out for mercy. When he had finished, she was gasping for breath. She struggled away from him and tried to tidy her hair with a shaking hand.

'Don't touch your hair,' he murmured, 'it suits you

166

better when it's untidy.' His satisfied half-smile and slitted eyes embarrassed her and she picked her way across his extended legs, carefully this time, to get at the food. He watched as she opened his rucksack, but made no comment. She threw him a packet of sandwiches, which he deftly caught, took a packet for herself and started eating them.

All the time there was the distant rushing of the falls, drowning the silence between them. No one else came along. She found the vacuum flask, poured some milk into the plastic cups and filled them with tea. 'I can't find the sugar,' she told him.

He searched deep down in his rucksack, without success and tutted irritably. 'Mother must have forgotten to put it in.'

'I think I've got some.' She delved into her rucksack and pulled out her belongings one after the other. 'It must be at the very bottom.'

Adrian sat up and dived towards the pile of clothes beside her. His hand closed on something soft and he held high his prize. 'They call this nightwear,' he teased, and grinned at her wickedly. 'I noticed this morning what a *thick* nightdress you were wearing.'

She tried to grab it, but he held her off. 'Very clever, these creations. It's not so much what they reveal as what they half reveal.' He ran the filmy garment through his fingers and looked at her provocatively. 'I realized this morning just how – potent they were.'

He held it tantalizingly high with one hand and held her groping arms away with the other. 'Even the scenery looks more attractive through it. Rose-coloured.' He let it float down into a pile of gossamer lightness and she snatched at it and stuffed it away. She found the jar of lump sugar and dropped two pieces into each cup.

'Anyway,' he mused, 'there seems little point in wearing such inviting night attire – when you *sleep alone*.'

Her eyes drew back from the cynicism in his. She knew what he was implying and refused to respond to his taunt. At last they finished their lunch and packed away the boxes and flask. Then they relaxed on the grass, side by side, and Adrian was so quiet, Rosalie thought he must be asleep.

Into the peace and stillness he thrust words which thundered their message into her brain. 'So Wallis Mason finally got what he wanted.'

She sat up. 'What do you mean?'

'I mean that he got you where he wanted you, in the end.'

'I'm sorry.' Her voice dripped ice. 'I may seem dim, but I still don't know what you're talking about.'

He raised himself on to his elbow and said in clear, concise tones, 'That he finally overcame your scruples, your principles, your moral objections, call them what you will, they all amount to the same thing – your resistance, and got what he wanted from you.' His eyes turned Arctic cold. 'Now do you understand? Or do I have to be brutally clear and spell it out in crude but unmistakable terms?'

She stared at him. 'So that's what you've been thinking all these hours I've spent with you and your mother?'

'You'd be surprised what I've been thinking. But can you blame me? According to your mother, you went to his house on the Friday evening after the episode at the dance, and again the next day. It's quite plain to me you're so much under his spell you can't keep away from the man. How could you bear to be parted from him for your two weeks' holiday?'

He plainly took her stunned silence as an admission of guilt, so he went on even more bitterly, 'I notice you don't deny it. Perhaps you even resented my dragging you from his arms that night in the staff room, in spite of the fact that he was being so brutish to you.'

Anger moved her so fast, she did not stop to think. While he watched, she collected all her belongings, pulled on her rucksack and walked off.

'You won't get far,' he called. 'There's no bus for hours, it's too far to walk and you can't take my car because you haven't got the ignition key.'

She walked across the bridge, her heart in her mouth, and when she reached the other side, she walked resolutely on. She did not know where she was going, nor did she care. She just had to get away from his taunts, his insults and the misery he was churning up in her heart. She crossed the stile and stopped, realizing then how hopeless it was trying to escape from him. She had to rely on his car to take her to Darlington. She was quite lost without him.

She dragged off her rucksack, threw herself face down on the grass in the shelter of the drystone wall, rested her face on her arms and cried her heart out. She was not aware of the passing of time, of how long she stayed like that. In between sobs, she realized that Adrian was leaning over her. He touched her shoulder.

'Rosalie, if I was wrong, I take back every word I said.'

She lay still. 'Rosalie,' he said softly, 'tell me. Do I take back my words?'

She raised her head slightly and nodded.

'So I was wrong.' He turned her over gently and she sat up. He found his handkerchief and wiped her eyes. 'Take it, use it yourself. You can return it some other time.' He held her chin and probed deep into her eyes. 'Tell me, I must know. Have you finished with him now?'

She shook her head and looked at him, imploring him to understand. 'There's still Melanie, Adrian. I can't break away because of her.'

'I see.' His tone was grim, his eyes withdrawn. She stood up, smoothed her slacks, tucked in her tee-shirt. He took her hand. 'Rosalie, this is a day on its own. Let's forget everything else and enjoy it as it comes. It's part of your holiday and I don't want to spoil it for you.'

She nodded and groped in her bag for a comb and compact. When she had repaired the damage which her tears had left behind, she felt better, but subdued. He helped her on with her rucksack, took her hand and walked her across the field and back to the car. He put their baggage in the boot.

'We won't need those next stop. If we'd had more time, we could have tried to find the stretch of the Pennine Way which runs from Winch Bridge to High Force. I did attempt the walk a few years ago, but somehow lost the track in the undergrowth and had to turn back.'

They soon covered the few miles between stops and Adrian turned the car into the hotel car park. They walked across the road, went through a small gate and paid the entrance fee to a man in a wooden hut.

Adrian told her, 'You can buy postcards on the way back, if you like.'

They walked along a winding wooded path with railings along one side, placed there as a safety measure to protect walkers from the steep tree-studded slope which fell away to the river Tees below. They turned a corner and Rosalie gasped. There, in the distance, in all its shining cascading beauty, was the Force itself.

Adrian smiled and gripped her hand. 'I was waiting for that. I knew exactly what your reaction would be when you first saw it. Everyone's the same. As you get nearer, you'll hear it, and close up the noise becomes a roar.' They moved on. 'I'll take you to the top of it, where you can look down on the fall itself.'

She was astonished. 'You can actually walk over the top?'

'Yes, and at times, when the river is very low, in drought conditions, it's possible to use stepping stones and cross to the other side of the river.'

On the way, they passed other people who were coming back from the waterfall. Then they were there. 'You can hear what I mean about the noise,' Adrian said, in her ear.

They stood and watched, and she caught her breath as the splashing, foaming wall of water threw itself over the ledge to the boulders seventy feet below. A great rock, vertically jointed, divided the fall into two. 'In full flood, when there has been extremely heavy rain,' Adrian told her, 'the water covers the entire area, and the two falls – the larger and the smaller – merge into one gigantic downpouring of water. But that's rare indeed. See,' he pointed upwards to the wall of rock in the middle, 'that's where we're going. You can see people up there, if you look carefully.'

'Is it really safe?' she wanted to know.

'If you behave sensibly and don't do anything foolish, yes.'

The steps to the top of the falls were steep and twisting, with a wooden rail on one side. Adrian led the way, striding up them with ease, leaving Rosalie puffing behind. He was laughing when she reached the top and put his arm round her. 'Along this path, through the gate and we're there.'

One or two other people were walking around. Adrian warned her to be careful where she put her feet, as there were pools in small hollows of the jagged, uneven rocks, and her shoes slipped over them as she clambered after him. He waited for her and took her hand to help her climb nearer the summit, so that they could look down on the waterfall itself. Then she saw it, and held her breath.

The noise was incessant and deafening and there could be no conversation. Not even a shout would carry over that unbelievable roar. As she watched the magnificent, terrifying sight, she knew she had never felt so alone in her life. She stared mindlessly at the deep, dark water as it swirled to the edge and plunged downwards. There was a bouncing glimpse below of the churning white foam, stained brown from the peat high in the hills.

'If I flowed with the water,' she thought, 'and hurled splashing, crashing down into that tumultuous froth, would I be cleansed of the guilt which I don't feel but which others tell me I should feel? Would I be freed from the entanglement with the child which has entwined itself round my willpower and robbed me of all ability to break away?'

As she gazed at the fast-moving river gaining speed and racing to the edge of the rock, all reality was shut out by the deafening, unceasing roar, and she became mesmerized, seeing down there the answer to all her problems. She swayed and instinctively groped at her side for an anchor. There came an agonized shout above the thundering water – 'Rosalie!'

Arms gripped her and pulled her back, and she turned

her face against a broad, hard chest, and clung with all her might. He led her to safety, found a flat rock, pushed her down and sat beside her. He raised his hand to smooth her hair, and she saw that it was shaking.

'I'm sorry, I'm so sorry,' she mumbled, 'I don't know what happened.'

He did not speak until he had composed himself. Then, 'Nothing happened, my love, nothing really happened at all.'

But he held her as if he would never let her go. He held her until they both became calmer, and then they smiled into each other's eyes. They kissed, and it was a giving and a taking by both of them, a kiss of equality willingly exchanged. They sat quietly, holding each other, in perfect accord, looking at the scenery around them.

The great chasm in the distance, through which the river flowed, was softened and mellowed by conifers and shrubs clinging valiantly to the eroded walls of rock. Behind them the river again, on a higher level, and as a magnificent, sombre backcloth, Mickle Fell rose forbiddingly to well over two thousand feet.

Rosalie touched Adrian's arm. 'There are two people over there who keep looking at us.'

'I know, I've seen them. They're neighbours of my mother. Jim Gill and his wife, next door but one.'

'Where the telephone is?' Adrian nodded. 'Then I must have spoken to him when I phoned your mother when you were ill.'

'You probably did. Want to be introduced?' He pulled her up, his arm still round her.

She tried to move away from him. 'Adrian, they might think. . . .'

'Let them think.'

'But they'll tell your mother.'

'Let them. It'll satisfy her grand-maternal longings, won't it?'

'But it will be such a disappointment to her when you tell her the truth.' Again she tried to pull away, but he held her tightly.

'Hallo there, Mr. Gill. Enjoying the view?'

The man raised his hand at Adrian's greeting, and helped his wife down from the rock they were standing on. 'Why, hallo, Adrian. How are you?' The couple studied Rosalie with some curiosity.

'A friend of mine, Rosalie Parham.' They shook hands. 'Rosalie claims to have made your acquaintance before by speaking to you on the telephone. Some weeks ago she phoned my mother—'

'Ah, I remember.' Jim's broad Yorkshire voice was pleasing and warm. 'Nice young lady you sounded, and I said so to my wife.'

Rosalie thanked him.

'On holiday, Miss—?'

'This is part of it, yes. I only came yesterday.'

'She's off tonight, unfortunately,' Adrian told him, pulling Rosalie closer and looking at her with affection in his eyes. 'Don't overact,' she wanted desperately to tell him. 'There's no need to overdo it.' 'She's in the middle of a walking tour,' he was saying, 'and she's joining a girl-friend in Darlington.'

'So you've got to make the most of the time, eh?' Mrs. Gill teased gently. They laughed and moved on. Mr. Gill called over his shoulder, 'Nice to see you going steady at last, Adrian. Your mother'll be pleased, I'll bet.'

'I told you, Adrian.' Her worried frown seemed to amuse him.

He smiled provocatively. 'Like Mrs. Fields, we'll let them keep their illusions a little longer, shall we?'

He helped her over the rocks to the gate, and they went down the steps to the lower path, running this time, and Rosalie arrived first. Hand-in-hand, they walked back to the road. She bought some postcards from the man in the wooden hut; some she intended to keep, some she would send to her friends.

They had tea at the hotel, a good, substantial meal, and when they had finished, Rosalie told Adrian that if she had eaten much more she would have had to loosen her belt, if she had been wearing one!

'Just what my mother ordered,' he said, then he looked at his watch and frowned. 'Time we were on our way.' He paid the bill and they walked to the car park. There were only two other cars parked there, and one of those belonged to Jim Gill, Adrian said. They got in the car.

'Thank you, Adrian, for a lovely day. I won't forget it, ever.'

They were quite alone. He looked at her searchingly, then took her in his arms. 'I'm going to say good-bye to you now, Rosalie.'

With their kiss, they seemed to join and merge into something beyond themselves. She rested her head against him. 'When will you be coming south again?'

'I planned to stay until the beginning of next term.'

She sat up, aghast. 'Five more weeks?'

He nodded and reached for the ignition key. How could she bear it? she asked herself. And at the end of those five weeks – what then? Nothing. Nothing more than she had ever had – her love for him. 'Women?' he had said once. 'I keep them out. I'm woman-proof.' Well, she had been warned.

For most of the journey to Darlington, they were silent. Adrian seemed preoccupied, unwilling to talk on any subject. They entered the town and he drove into a car park not far from the town centre.

'We're a little earlier than I intended. Where are you meeting Marion?'

'Outside the hotel where we're staying the night.'

'Where are you going tomorrow?'

'To Durham, to look around the city. We'll be there a couple of nights. After that, we go south to York for an overnight stop. We'll arrive home late on Monday.'

'Then what?'

She shrugged, avoiding his eyes. 'I don't know. There are various – matters I must attend to.'

'Must?' His eyes darkened. 'There's no "must" about it, is there? It's another person's problem, not yours.'

She felt bleak, hopeless. 'Adrian, it's a commitment I must honour. I cannot let the child down. I – I shouldn't tell you this, but Wallis has contacted his solicitor and asked him to trace his wife.'

'That's simply a smoke-screen, Rosalie, to fool you into

believing he's on the level.'

'But I'm sure he's serious about getting her back, not so much for his own sake, judging by what he's told me, but for his daughter's.'

His lips tightened. 'So he's got as far as discussing his wife with you, has he?'

She was silent. She could not tell him about Wallis's unhappy married life because it would be betraying his trust.

'I suppose,' Adrian persisted, with a cynical smile, 'he told you his wife didn't "understand him", to put it in conventional, old-fashioned terms.'

She glanced at him sharply, giving herself away by her surprise.

'I thought so. And you were taken in by that?' He shook his head sadly. 'I give you up.'

'It's no use, Adrian.' Her throat was dry, lips stiff. 'I repeat, I can't, I simply cannot let the child down.' She held out her hand. 'Good-bye, Adrian. Thank you for today. That at least I shall never forget.'

He ignored her hand. 'Don't forget your luggage,' was all he said.

She took her things and got out, looked vaguely round, feeling utterly lost. 'Good-bye, Adrian,' she repeated.

'Good-bye, Rosalie.'

She walked away, out of the car park and along the street. She did not turn. She didn't care where she was going, but assumed it was in the right direction. She went on blindly. She felt as though she had plunged headlong over High Force into that turbulent chasm, and was floundering and struggling for her very life. That anguished cry rang again in her ears. She heard it clearly. *'Rosalie!'*

She turned her head, frantically seeking for his car. It had gone. The waters closed over her head and she was sucked down to the depths at last.

CHAPTER TEN

THE next few days passed somehow. Rosalie was determined not to let Marion even begin to guess at her deep unhappiness. But the effort of appearing bright and cheerful and displaying an intelligent interest in everything they saw exhausted her, and when she arrived home on Monday evening, she felt almost ill. With her parents away, the quietness of the house unnerved her.

The following day she telephoned Wallis to ask him if Melanie was home from her grandmother's house. He said he was going to collect her the next day, but would Rosalie please go and cheer him up that evening? She refused, and nothing he could say would make her alter her mind.

He suggested that on the Thursday, which would be Melanie's first day at home, he might take the three of them to the sea. Did she like the idea?

Rosalie said she did. 'Shall we take a picnic lunch? I'll make the sandwiches.'

He arranged to pick her up early that morning. He was determined to take them out, he said, come rain or shine.

To fill the empty hours between and to stop herself brooding about Adrian, she prepared several pages of notes for next term's lectures. Nichol telephoned the following day and told her that he and Jane were unofficially engaged.

'I'm delighted to hear it, Nichol. Let me know when it's official and I'll buy you both an engagement present.' He promised he would and rang off.

The day Rosalie spent with Wallis and Melanie was warm and sunny. She splashed about in the sea with Melanie and they made sandcastles and shell patterns and lay in the sunshine and relaxed. Wallis hardly stirred from his place beside their clothes. He seemed subdued, preoccupied.

'Anything wrong, Wallis?'

He drew his knees up to his chin, and rested his arms on them. 'I have my problems.' His eyes travelled over her as she lay beside him in her swimsuit, and he laughed. 'The sight of you, appetizing and inviting as you are, is one of my biggest.'

She sat up, feeling ridiculously guilty. She wanted to apologize and said so. They laughed together, then he became serious. 'Rosalie, when we get back, I'd like to talk to you. Would you – agree to have a drink with me when Melanie is in bed?'

'I – I don't know, Wallis. . . .'

'Please, Rosalie. You have nothing to fear from me – now.'

So she agreed. 'It's time we were going, anyway.'

She called Melanie back to dry herself and dress, and together they changed from their damp swimsuits into their clothes, hiding under the large towels.

On the way home, they stopped for tea. They were late back and Rosalie bundled a weary little girl into bed almost immediately. Then she joined Wallis in the lounge. He gave her a drink and sat beside her on the couch.

He studied the golden brown liquid in his glass. 'You probably remember I told you I'd decided to try to find my wife?'

She nodded. 'Has she – have you managed to—'

He held up his hand, then put it over hers. 'You're going too fast. My solicitor has traced her whereabouts and has given me an address. He suggests I try to see her there.' He stopped, moved Rosalie's hand on to his knee and stroked it. She tensed and was about to remove it when he said, 'I was thinking of going tomorrow and I was wondering if I could impose on your good nature further and ask you to have Melanie while I'm away. I may not be back until late, whether or not I return alone. My wife's reaction to my suggestion that we – er – get together again is, of course, an unknown quantity. There has been no contact or communication between us since she went away.'

'Yes, of course I'll have Melanie tomorrow. I could take her out for the day, to London perhaps, if you've no objection.'

'Take her where you like. I'll pay all expenses, of course.' He lifted her fingers to his lips and she was so pleased to hear his news, she allowed him to do it. 'Thank you, Rosalie, for helping me out. I appreciate it more than I can say.' He pulled her towards him, but she held back.

'You want me to trust you, Wallis.'

'Sorry, Rosalie. You're too darned attractive for any man to resist.'

But Rosalie told herself she knew differently. One man had proved completely resistant. She found her handbag and jacket.

'I must go.'

Wallis took her home and dropped her at the gate. 'I'll be leaving early in the morning, so expect my daughter before nine.'

'I'll be ready, Wallis. Thanks for the lovely day.'

'Thanks for coming. I – I shall miss you, Rosalie.' He looked at her for a long moment, raised his hand and drove away.

As she let herself into the house, depression welcomed her in. It was everywhere. The pretence of cheerfulness, of seeming to enjoy every moment had weighed her down all day. Now no pretence was necessary, and she sank into an armchair and gave herself up to her misery. The stillness of the house was almost tangible. The emptiness was all around her, and the void inside her was a pain she could not cure. She looked at her watch. Time for bed. She had spent much longer with Wallis than she had intended.

The telephone shattered the silence. She waited a moment before crossing the hall to answer it. For some strange reason, she was almost afraid. 'It must be Wallis about tomorrow,' she thought.

She lifted the receiver. 'Rosalie?' the telephone nearly clattered to the floor. Adrian? It couldn't be. She did not answer because she knew it was her imagination tricking her. She felt she could cry out with disappointment.

The voice came again. 'Rosalie! Are you there?'

'Is that – is that Adrian?' She spoke in a whisper.

'Yes, this *is* Adrian. You're in at last! I've been trying to contact you for hours.'

'I've been out all day with—'

'Rosalie, I've come south for a few days to see the publishers about the book. I – I want to see you tomorrow before I go to town. Or when I come back. It's up to you.'

Tomorrow? It would have to be tomorrow. 'Oh, Adrian, I'm so sorry. I'll be out all day. I'm taking Melanie to London.' Tears of defeat inched their way down her cheeks.

'I see. I should have known. So that's that.' There was a heavy silence. 'Are you – are you all going together, all three of you? Or,' a note of hope lifted his voice, 'just the two of you?'

'The two of us. Her father's going out for the day. Adrian, he's going to try to find his wife.'

Another pause, then, 'I was wondering – could I come with you?'

'Come with us?' How could she keep the joy from her voice? She did not even try. 'Oh, Adrian, I'd be delighted if you would. It's – it's quite a responsibility for me to take someone else's child all that way on my own.'

'Then I'll come. I'll pick you up in my car and we'll drive to the station, travel to London by train and I'll leave you there for a couple of hours while you go sightseeing, and rejoin you for lunch. Does that suit you?'

'Wonderful, Adrian.' They arranged a time, and she asked after his mother.

'I told her I would be seeing you and she sends her love.' His voice altered subtly. 'She insisted that I must deliver it to you in person.'

Rosalie was sure he could hear her heartbeats. 'Is the – is the package it's wrapped in attractive?'

'That depends on the eye of the beholder, so we shall just have to wait and see, won't we?' She could hear that he was smiling. 'Till tomorrow, Rosalie. Good night.'

She answered him in a whisper and replaced the receiver with a shaking hand. Now the house shouted at her with joy, now the ache inside her had gone. Life was flowing round her again, and it was taking her on a tide of happiness towards tomorrow.

Melanie arrived early. Wallis watched as Rosalie let her into the house, waved and was gone. Melanie was dancing with unrestrained joy. When she heard that Adrian was going with them, she hugged Rosalie to the point of choking her, and skipped into the garden to play while Rosalie changed. She decided to wear a new deep pink dress. It was sleeveless and round-necked and it moulded itself to her figure in a flattering way. Her handbag and shoes were white and she combed her hair softly round her face. She used only a light covering of make-up. She wanted so desperately to please Adrian.

He arrived on time. He came into the hall and held out his gift. 'One transistor radio, as promised.'

Rosalie gazed at it. 'How can I thank you?'

'That's easy. Come into the lounge and I'll show you how.'

She put the radio on the table and twiddled a knob. It worked at once, loud and clear. Adrian explained the function of the various controls and how to select the different stations and wavelengths.

He stood behind her and wrapped his arms about her.

'Now thank me for being a good boy and giving it to you.'

She turned and reached up to kiss him. 'Like the touch-down of a butterfly,' he said, and pulled her to him. 'Now I'll give you my mother's love and when you see her again, you can tell her what a good son I am.' His kiss was hard, prolonged and very thorough, and she wanted it to go on and on. 'No soft landing about that,' he said, when he had finished.

She stood for a moment within his arms, just drinking in the details about his face that she had tried so hard to remember in the long dark hours since she had last seen him. He ran his forefinger over her eyebrows and traced the curve of her lips, then he kissed her again.

They drew apart and when he turned his head without releasing her, she followed his eyes. Melanie was staring at them, uncertain and frowning. She pulled at Rosalie's dress. 'Now you kiss me like you've just kissed your brother.'

Rosalie unwound herself from Adrian and hugged the little girl, kissing her gently on both cheeks, and Melanie played with her hair. 'Do you love me like you love your brother?'

'He's not my—'

'You haven't answered the young lady's question, Rosalie.' Adrian was laughing, and Rosalie's confusion increased.

'Of course I love you, Melanie.'

Adrian said again, 'You still haven't answered. . . .'

'When are we going?' Melanie wanted to know.

'When I've locked up and put on some more powder. Are you ready?' Melanie nodded.

'And you, Adrian?'

'I'm ready for anything, Rosalie.'

She ignored his teasing and ran upstairs to renew her make-up. Then they were ready to go.

The train journey took nearly an hour. Rosalie had bought some comics for Melanie to read. She sat next to her, while Adrian sat opposite them both. Rosalie tried to concentrate on the paperback she had brought with her, but her eyes kept wandering to Adrian over the other side. He was reading a newspaper and now and then their eyes met over the top of the pages, and then Rosalie would look away, embarrassed. After a while, he moved his briefcase from the rack above him to the one above Rosalie's head, then he sat beside her.

He smiled and drew her arm through his. 'This is much more comfortable,' he whispered. She gave up all pretence of reading and closed her eyes and wallowed in her dreams. When the train drew into the London terminus, she shook herself back to reality. Adrian pulled his case from the rack and joined them on the platform.

'You're going to the Tower, aren't you?'

Melanie clapped her hands. 'The Tower of London?'

'Yes. Would you like that?'

She was too excited to speak. They walked together along the platform and through the barrier and Melanie stayed close to Rosalie's side, afraid of the jostling crowds that pushed past all the time.

Adrian gripped Rosalie's hand. 'I'll meet you at the Tower gates, one o'clock sharp.'

''Bye, Adrian!' Melanie waved frantically, eager to be off.

Adrian touched Rosalie's lips with his, then she watched until he was drawn away and lost in the shifting patterns of the crowds. She tried to revive her drooping spirits by telling herself that in less than three hours she would be seeing him again. She took Melanie's hand and they went down the steps to the Underground station. It was a new experience for Melanie and she stared open-eyed at the sliding doors, the brightness of the stations and the darkness of the tunnels.

When they climbed the stairs to the street and walked into the daylight, she blinked and danced along at Rosalie's side. They had to join the queue to get inside the Tower grounds. After that, Melanie would not let Rosalie rest until she had seen almost everything, including waiting for over half an hour in a long, slow-moving queue to see the Crown Jewels.

By the end of the morning, Rosalie was the one who was flagging, and it was Melanie who was skipping with energy. But when they returned to the entrance at the appointed time, and Rosalie saw Adrian waiting there, the life flowed back into her body and she wanted to skip like Melanie.

They walked along the street looking for a restaurant for lunch and found one which suited their tastes and their pockets. Afterwards they went to Trafalgar Square. Melanie gazed, full of awe, to the top of Nelson's column, watched the cascading water of the fountains, made friends with the pigeons and talked to the great sculptured lions as though they were living creatures. Later, they ate ice creams, sitting on a bench with Melanie between them.

'It's years since I did this,' Adrian commented. 'Not since I was a boy, in fact.' He smiled at Rosalie over Melanie's head. 'It makes a pleasant change, in the right company.'

Melanie looked up and caught them smiling at each other. 'Do you love your brother?' she asked Rosalie.

'Adrian's not my brother, Melanie.'

She frowned. 'But he loves you, so he must be your brother.'

'Anyway, not all sisters love their brothers,' Rosalie told her, dodging the issue.

'But if I had one,' she persisted, a little desperately, 'I know I would love him. So you *must* love your brother. Do you?' Her large eyes turned to Rosalie's, pleading for the right answer.

'Yes, all right, Melanie. I do love my brother.' She could not bring herself to look at Adrian.

Melanie sighed happily, her tenuous and dwindling faith in the unity of the family temporarily restored.

'Miss Parham,' came a voice from her other side, 'remind me to have a long and urgent discussion with you later, in more – er – appropriate circumstances, about brotherly – and sisterly – love.' The expression in his eyes made her pulse rate double.

At the end of the day, Melanie was so exhausted she went to sleep in the train with her head resting against Rosalie's arm, hugging the doll Adrian had bought her. Adrian sat next to Rosalie too, holding her close.

It was well past Melanie's bedtime when the train drew into the station. She awoke with a start when Adrian lifted her down to the platform. Rosalie followed, carrying his briefcase.

'Soon be home,' he told Melanie, as she put one hand in his and the other in Rosalie's. She emerged from her daze in the cool evening air, and they swung her high and low between them as they walked to the station car park.

Adrian slowed down and stopped at the kerb outside

Melanie's house. 'So Wallis is home.' Rosalie was surprised to see his car in the garage. Melanie got out and Rosalie followed.

Adrian told her sharply, 'Come straight back, Rosalie. Her father will have to put her to bed.'

'But, Adrian—'

His voice was dangerously quiet. 'You heard what I said. You will come – straight – back. You cannot, repeat cannot, stay.'

She turned from the car window and caught Melanie up at the front door. Through the uncurtained window Rosalie saw two people side by side on the couch. She crouched down and put her arms round Melanie, kissing her for the last time.

'Good night, darling,' she said. 'I'll leave you now. You've got a – a lovely surprise waiting for you inside your house. You won't need me any more.'

Melanie kissed her back. Then Rosalie rang the bell, but did not wait for the door to be opened. She ran all the way back to Adrian's car and turned, as they were driving away, to see Melanie being welcomed in.

Adrian gave her a few moments to recover, then he said, 'Well?'

'Well?' She knew her tone was belligerent. 'You may like to know that, despite your disbelief, Wallis's wife has gone back to him.'

He sighed loudly. 'Thank God for that! Now perhaps that incredibly powerful sense of duty which is a maddening part of your personality will let you rest in peace.'

Rosalie was silent, lowering her head to the back of the seat and closing her eyelids tightly against the tears.

Adrian opened the front door with his key. He propelled her into the lounge. 'Sit down. I'll get some coffee. It's obvious you're suffering from an emotional shock. You need reviving.'

They drank the coffee in silence. Then she leaned back in the armchair, while Adrian half-sprawled on the couch, watching her through half-closed, slightly sardonic eyes.

'So,' he said, 'it's over. And you've come out of the encounter unscathed. I don't think you realize what a narrow escape you've had. You're the one that got away. That must have annoyed Mason. His last fling, and it didn't come off.'

'Cynical to the last, aren't you?' She stood up. She was acutely aware of him and wandered aimlessly round the room, trying to work the feeling off.

He went on talking in the same provocative tone. 'Duty has been done, your conscience is clear and you're free at last of the Wallis Mason tentacles. And still in one piece?'

She frowned. What was he getting at?

'Heart-whole and fancy free, Rosalie?' he asked softly. 'Overflowing with sisterly love for me, as you told Melanie?' A ghost of a smile haunted his lips. 'If so, I'm sorry, because I haven't an atom of brotherly love in me for you.'

She frowned again. What was the matter with him? But, she argued, what had she expected – a declaration of love, a proposal of marriage? From a man who had made it crystal clear at the beginning of their acquaintance that no woman could ever hold a permanent place in his life? He was, in his own words, 'woman-proof'. He was a man out of reach.

He stood up, slowly straightened himself to his full height. He said, quietly, compellingly, 'Come here, Rosalie.'

She walked across the room and stood in front of him. His hands were deep in his trouser pockets and she tolerated his eyes as they moved indolently over her. 'Recovered your balance yet?'

She knew he was referring to her parting from Melanie, the division of their lives. She nodded.

His whole body tensed and he spoke quickly. 'That's just as well, because I'm now going to knock you off it again.'

He whipped his hands from his pockets and before she could take a breath, his arms had her yielding body in a suffocating grip. The pressure of his mouth forced back

185

her head and his lips went about their business with breathtaking efficiency. When he had had enough, she was panting. She pressed her cheek against his chest. His voice was muffled as he murmured into her hair, 'If that hasn't convinced you that I love you,' he held her away, 'then I shall have to take more potent action.' He caught at her chin and pulled her face round. 'Look at me, darling, let me see those lovely eyes.'

She looked at him and he whispered, as if to himself, 'Yes, the message is there, loud and clear. You love me?'

She gave him his answer over and over again, until his lips cut off the words.

'You'll have to marry me, darling,' he murmured against the hollow of her neck. 'When you left me at Darlington, I felt as though I'd lost a vital part of my body. I had to come south – I couldn't keep away from you.' He whispered against her mouth, 'I'm only half alive without you.' After a long time he said, abstractedly, between kisses, 'You'll be marrying a mathematician. Does that worry you?'

She shook her head. 'I've got conditioned to them. I cut my milk teeth on mathematical formulae. One more in the family? I can take it.' She snuggled close. 'Especially this one.'

'I'll teach you maths, sweetheart. I promised I would, didn't I?'

She nodded dreamily. 'Just as long as I can sit on your knee while you teach me.'

He laughed. 'Now that's a novel place for a student to sit – on the lecturer's knee. But I'm more than willing to try it out.'

He sat down and pulled her down on to his lap. 'I'll tell you a story. Are you sitting comfortably?' She nodded. 'There was a girl called Rosalie. One day, she pushed her way into my flat. She had the audacity to invite herself in where no other young woman had been allowed to tread. Then, days, or it may have been hours, later, she pushed her way into my thoughts, then in no time at all, into my heart. Now she's pushed herself into my very life and I find I can't live without her. I won't have a moment's peace until she's my wife.'

'More than anything else in the world, Adrian,' she whispered, just before his mouth stopped her talking for a long, long time, 'I want to be your wife.'

He murmured at last, 'I'm not giving you long, sweetheart. A couple of days. . . .'

She was aghast. 'But, Adrian—'

'I'm warning you, my darling, if you try to keep me waiting, I'll break all the rules. I'll move in with you and—'

She gave in. Next day, while Adrian obtained the special licence, Rosalie went shopping and bought herself a dress and jacket in palest blue. She chose a small white hat and accessories to match, then together they bought the ring.

Two days later, they were married. Nichol and Jane were there. Rosalie had telephoned Nichol to tell him the news and invited them both to attend the ceremony at the local registrar's office and act as witnesses. Afterwards, they all went to lunch at a large and expensive hotel in the town, where they toasted each other in the best champagne.

On the way back to the house, Rosalie and Adrian called on Mrs. Fields and told her what they had done. She kissed them both and, with tears in her eyes, and her face wreathed in smiles, she waved them off.

For the rest of the holiday, Adrian moved in with Rosalie. One day, in one of their saner moments, he pulled her on to his knee. The summer holidays were nearing their end and the beginning of the new term was approaching.

'My beautiful wife,' he said, 'it's time we acknowledged the existence of the outside world and told some of our relatives what we've done, otherwise they might find out somehow that we're living together and put the worst construction on it. And that would never do, would it?'

She traced the line of his lips, then kissed them. 'So what do you suggest, darling?'

187

'That we send telegrams in all directions, across the world if necessary, regardless of cost. Then everyone will be happy.'

So they used the telephone and sent a cable to her parents in the south of France. 'Have got married,' it said. 'Could not wait for your return. Hope you understand and approve. Love, Rosalie, Adrian.'

Then they sent a telegram to Adrian's mother. 'Have got married. We know you will approve. Expect us any time for a short honeymoon. Love, Adrian, Rosalie.'

Somehow Rosalie had pushed herself into Adrian's arms and he replaced the receiver and gazed down at her. 'Now you've got two mothers. And both of them love you. Satisfied, Mrs. Crayford?'

'Very satisfied, my darling husband. Very satisfied indeed.'

She wound her arms round his neck and held up her mouth for his kiss.

Mills & Boon Classics

The very best of Mills & Boon
romances, brought back for those
of you who missed reading them
when they were first published.

and in
February
we bring back the following four
great romantic titles

THE CASTLE IN THE TREES by *Rachel Lindsay*
The very name of the Castle in the Trees fascinated
Stephanie, and the reality was even more intriguing than
she had imagined. But there was mystery there too. Why
did Miguel and Carlos de Maroc hate each other? Stephanie
found out at last, but only at the cost of losing her heart.

ISLAND OF PEARLS by *Margaret Rome*
Many English girls go to Majorca for their holiday in the secret
hope of meeting romance. Hazel Brown went there and found
a husband. But she was not as romantically lucky as she
appeared to be — for Hazel's was a husband with a difference...

THE SHROUDED WEB by *Anne Mather*
For several very good reasons Justina wished to keep the news
of her husband's death from her frail, elderly aunt. Then she
heard of the Englishman Dominic Hallam, who was in hospital
suffering from amnesia, and the germ of an idea came into
her mind...

DEVIL IN A SILVER ROOM by *Violet Winspear*
Margo Jones had once loved Michel, so when he died she
found herself going to look after his small son in the French
chateau of Satancourt. There Margo met Paul Cassilis, Michel's
inscrutable brother, to whom women were just playthings,
but in "Miss Jones" was to find one woman who was determined not to be.

If you have difficulty in obtaining any of these titles through
your local paperback retailer, write to:

Mills & Boon Reader Service
P.O. Box 236, Thornton Road, Croydon, Surrey, CR9 3RU.

The Mills & Boon Rose is the Rose of Romance

Every month there are ten new titles to choose from — ten
new stories about people falling in love, people you want to
read about, people in exciting, far away places. Choose Mills
& Boon. It's your way of relaxing.

January's titles are:

BED OF GRASS by Janet Dailey
Judd Prescott had been the reason for Valerie leaving home.
Now she was back, but Judd still didn't know what that
reason had been . . .

WINTER WEDDING by Betty Neels
Professor Renier Jurres-Romeijn regarded Emily as a 'prim
miss'. So it wasn't surprising that he so obviously preferred her
lively sister Louise.

DANGEROUS DECEPTION by Lilian Peake
Anona Willis was engaged to the forceful Shane Brodie — but
he had admitted that he had no staying power where women
were concerned . . .

FEVER by Charlotte Lamb
The attraction between Sara Nichols and Nick Rawdon was
immediate — but somehow Sara could never clear up the
misunderstanding about her stepbrother Greg.

SWEET HARVEST by Kerry Allyne
Any thought of a reconciliation between herself and her
husband soon vanished when Alix realised that Kirby had
chosen her successor . . .

STAY THROUGH THE NIGHT by Flora Kidd
Virtually kidnapped aboard Burt Sharaton's yacht, Charlotte
was told that if she didn't co-operate with him, he would
ruin her father . . .

HELL OR HIGH WATER by Anne Mather
Jarret Manning was attractive, successful, experienced — and
Helen Chase felt mingled antagonism and fear every time she
met this disturbing man.

CANDLE IN THE WIND by Sally Wentworth
Shipwrecked, her memory lost, Sam had to believe her
companion Mike Scott when he told her she was his wife . . .

WHITE FIRE by Jan MacLean
Rana had fallen wildly in love with Heath Markland, to the
fury of her domineering mother. But perhaps she knew something about Heath that Rana didn't . . .

A STREAK OF GOLD by Daphne Clair
Eight years ago, Ric Burnett had cruelly told Glenna to get
out of his life — but now they had met again . . .

If you have difficulty in obtaining any of these books
from your local paperback retailer, write to:

Mills & Boon Reader Service
P.O. Box 236, Thornton Road, Croydon, Surrey, CR9 3RU

192

Masquerade
Historical Romances

Intrigue
excitement
romance

MOON OF LAUGHING FLAME
by Belinda Grey

Could Deborah forget her old, strict life in Victorian
England and become the obedient squaw of Adam-
Leap-The-Mountain — the arrogant half-breed brave
who was willing to kill to gain her?

THE ICE KING
by Dinah Dean

A season in St. Petersburg at the court of Czar
Alexander was Tanya's one chance of gaiety. Yet
she fell in love with Prince Nikolai — the Ice King —
a man of whom she knew nothing . . .

Look out for these titles in your local paperback shop from
11th January 1980